ANYTIME ANYWHERE

ANYTIME ANYWHERE

Camp Auschwitz

ROGER CORON

MH Coron Books

Acknowledgements:
I would like to thank my wonderful editor Julia King. Thank you
Nick Brown for your direction. Latte Goldstein created a beautiful
cover.

Thank you to my mom for instilling my love for reading.
Thank you to my wife, Radhika, for your love and support.
Thank you to my kids Mark and Hunter who have been my biggest
fans and supporters. Love you boys!
Also a big thank you to my GI team at TSC and TMC.

First Printing, 2024

I dedicate this book to the memory of the six million Jews who lost their lives during the Holocaust. World War II was the deadliest conflict in world history. Estimates of 75 million people around the world were killed during the war. Each of them had a life and a story and most of those stories will never be told.

Disclaimer

While inspired by real events and historical characters, this is a work of fiction and does not claim to be historically accurate or portray factual events or relationships. Please keep in mind that the references to actual persons, living or dead, business establishments, events or locales may not be factually accurate, but rather fictionalized by the author.

Prologue

Camp Ohiwa 1965

She raced through the brush, panting with exhaustion. Her face was stained with dirt and sweat. Her shorts were ripped along the right leg, and blood dripped down, leaving a trail behind. She could hear the boys' voices as they searched for her through bunk eleven. Laughing. Hooting.

A fury of crashing noises as the beds were overturned made Jessica jump. She ducked behind the bunk, peering around the corner to the open grassy field where the head of the camp was standing at attention in front of the cowering children, whistle in mouth and baton in hand. He eyed the children lined in rows. She could hear them calling out their numbers for roll call in frightened, quivering voices. When he marched out of sight, Jessica took the chance to break into the woods behind the bunk and head toward the nature trail leading to the lake.

The camp property abutted the lake, and several other camps could be seen miles across on the far side. Over there lay safety and salvation. If only she could find Bobby and Jonathan at the rendezvous point. She was set to meet them at the boat house along the lake, and from there they would escape, getting help at Camp Timber on the opposite side.

But as she continued to half run, half limp down the dirt trail, she could hear the boys' voices getting louder. They must have only been 200 yards behind her.

Crack! She stepped on a fallen branch, lost her footing, and tumbled over the side of the trail, rolling down the rocks, hitting her shoulder, then knee, and finally hearing a snap as her arm broke. She came to a rest at the base of the boat house. The pain was searing. Her head rolled to the right.

Through her cloudy, stinging tears, she could now see, staring back at her, the eyes of Jonathan's bloodied and dead body.

One

Berlin 1935

David woke up on a cool autumn day. He could smell coffee brewing and eggs and bacon frying on the stove. As he climbed out of bed, he smiled, feeling so proud to finally be a teenager. Today was his thirteenth birthday. Pushing his thick brown hair out of his eyes, he went to the sink to wash his face and clean his teeth.

Downstairs his mother was squeezing oranges. "Happy Birthday, David! Come here and give me a kiss."

David's mother, Barbara, was a beautiful woman. She was average height with long, flowing dirty-blonde hair that curled at the ends.

"The man of the hour!" announced his father in his deep voice. He was dressed in his dark banker's suit even though it was Saturday. He was sitting at the kitchen table reading *The Berliner Times*. "My dear boy, we are so proud of you! Thirteen. Where has the time gone? Just yesterday, your mother was changing your diapers, and now what's that? Is that some hair on your lip? Soon I will have to give you your first razor and teach you to shave."

"What are you reading?" David asked.

"Oh, just more of the same. Herr Hitler has continued to enact more race laws against the Jews."

"Good," David said. "They're filthy animals. They are so few and yet have all the money. They steal from honest working Germans."

"David, enough of that!" his mother scolded as she turned to look out the window. He felt his ears grow hot, feeling so ashamed to be scolded by his mother. He lowered his head and sat at the table. No one spoke.

"David, there is something I must tell you now. It's important," his father said, looking grim.

"No, not now," Mother asserted, regaining her composure.

"Barb, today David is a man, and he must know. David, come sit beside me. There is something we need to talk about."

Doing as he was asked, he sat down next to his father. His mother wiped her hands on her dish towel and sat beside David as well.

"David, there is no easy way to say it so I just will. I am Jewish."

David felt the blood drain from his face. He felt dizzy, and then nauseous. His father paused, and when David looked up, he continued. "When I met your mama at university in Austria, we were initially just friends. Of course, our relationship grew, and we eventually decided to get married. Mama knew that her father, your grandfather, was strongly involved in the rising Nazi party. Of course, it was not yet called that, but she knew how he felt about Jewish people. So, when we decided to get married, she said that when she introduced me to her parents, I would have to act as if I was a Christian. I was never very religious, and since I had no family of my own, I agreed. After all, your mama is the most beautiful and talented woman in the world. I would do anything for her. So, when we returned to Germany and decided to take up in Berlin, I left behind any traces of my Jewish origins. I left behind my real name, Harry Grossbaum, and instead became Fredrick Wagner."

"I have always felt bad that I made your papa make that choice," David's mother said quietly. "I decided that when you were of age, we would tell you and give you a Bar Mitzvah in secret. We did the same for Samuel two years ago."

David felt like his whole world was coming apart. Samuel, his older brother, was his role model. He was tall and blond like Mama and had her blue eyes. He was rising quickly in the Hitler Youth. *How could this be?* David thought.

"Now, of course, this must remain a secret," his father continued. "Today we will have a small ceremony at home with Aunt Jean and Uncle Barron. No one else knows. Even your cousin Eric doesn't know and should never find out. The only people who know I am Jewish are your mother's sister, Jean, and Barron Bauer, and us. Barron is my closest friend and I would trust him with my life."

"I don't want a Bar Mitzvah. I don't want to be Jewish. Why did you tell me?"

"David, there is nothing wrong with being Jewish. Hitler and the Nazi party have radical ideas and have used the Jews as a scapegoat for all of the economic trouble that Germany has faced. By blaming the Jews they have been able to secure political power," said Father.

"But it is their fault. They sneak around and take advantage of their fellow Germans."

"None of that is true," interjected Mother. "That is just the propaganda your father is talking about. The Jews are good people. They are no different than their Christian counterparts. Your father is the most kind and supportive man. And you, David, think of all your wonderful qualities and how well liked you are. Nothing has changed. You are still the same person."

"But because of the time we live in, for now we must keep our heritage a secret. In a few years Hitler will be gone and we can celebrate who we are," his father said.

Mama kissed David on the forehead. "Now, David, it's Saturday morning, so it's time to take your weekly bath. Go upstairs after breakfast, scrub yourself nice and clean, and then put on the clothes I have laid out for you. Today is going to be a big day."

When he finished his bacon and eggs, David jumped out of his seat and ran to the stairs. In general, David hated taking baths but now he looked forward to the time alone. Maybe he could soak away all of the anxiety and confusion from this new revelation. When the bathtub was filled, he closed and locked the door. He threw his clothes on the floor and climbed into the tub. Last week while washing, he noticed that his body was beginning to change. His legs were growing longer, and he could no longer extend them entirely in the tub. His body, while still scrawny, was becoming slightly more muscular, and he noticed the beginning of hair growing on his body. He was becoming a man and a Jew all at once.

With thoughts of confusion and despair, he sank lower in the tub and started to cry.

"David," called Mama, "don't forget to wash your armpits."

David thought more about Samuel. He missed his older brother. He was on a three-month training program arranged through the Hitler Youth program. How come his brother never told him about being Jewish? He felt so bad for him. What must it be like to be part of the Hitler Youth, which actively preached hatred toward the Jews? If anyone could handle it, though, it would be Samuel. He was always very good at everything in school. He was one of the most athletic children in his class. And he was tough. Tough as steel.

David thought back to the time his brother protected him from one of the schoolyard bullies last spring. One of Samuel's best friends was Josef Fefferhaussen. Josef, who was Samuel's age, was an amiable, caring boy who always seemed to keep himself above the fray. Josef had two brothers: Carl, who was fourteen at the time, and Anton, who was just nine. While you could always count on Josef, his younger brother Carl was a different story. Carl was one of those boys who despite being a year younger than Josef was two inches taller and very muscular. When he got angry, which was often, he would beat up on the smaller kids in the neighborhood.

One day after school, Samuel, David, Eric, Josef, Carl, and Anton were playing outside in front of David's house. This was not uncommon because Josef lived almost right across the street. As their game of tag ended, they decided to play a game of mercy. Mercy was a game where boys locked hands and twisted, making it uncomfortable for the other boy. You won the game when the other boy couldn't handle the pain anymore and shouted "mercy!" Carl, who was still fuming about being tagged by David, challenged David to the first match. The boys met in the center of the circle of friends and began. Carl easily took the early advantage over David, twisting his hand around and backward. David tried to be brave but the pain was intense. He thought his hands would break and after only about fifteen seconds of playing he was shouting for mercy. Instead of letting go, Carl continued to twist as David began to cry, shouting, "Mercy! Mercy! Mercy!"

Eric, Samuel, and Josef shouted for Carl to let go but to no avail. Anton looked on with excitement at his big brother hurting David.

Finally, Samuel jumped in, slapping Carl on the back. "Why don't you pick on someone your own size?"

With this, Carl released David, who dropped to a knee, rubbing his wrist to relieve the searing ache.

Even though Samuel was a couple of years older than Carl, he was not quite as big as him, but it was closer to a fair match. Knowing that he had little chance and wanting to avenge his little brother for what Carl had just done to him, Samuel cheated. The boys met in the middle of the circle. They interlocked hands. "One, two, three, start!"

Samuel, knowing he was not as strong as Carl, jumped up and used his full weight to come down and snap Carl's hands backward. Carl screamed "mercy!" and the match was over in less than two seconds.

David looked up at his brother with admiration in his eyes. Eric and Josef also looked on, happy to see the bully get his due. But the good feelings didn't last as Carl jumped to his feet. He had this look of rage in his eyes. His right eye even started to deviate away from the midline, giving him this psychotic appearance. "You're dead!" he said, pointing his finger at Samuel.

Carl took a step toward Samuel and began wildly swinging both arms with balled fists. He lunged at Samuel, who was able to duck under a right hook. The blow glanced off the top of Samuel's head without much impact. He used Carl's forward momentum to let him pass him. In a split second, Samuel managed to wrap his left arm around Carl's neck and turned, delivering an upper cut right into Carl's mouth. Carl stepped back as blood began to drip from his nose. He touched his face, and seeing the blood, turned and ran home. From that day on, David, his cousin Eric and even Carl's brothers Josef and Anton looked up to Samuel. He'd stood up to the big bully and punched him in the nose.

Back to the present, David thought that his brother would be all right. He was tough. He was his hero and he would handle whatever the Hitler Youth camp threw at him. He pulled himself out of the bath and began to dry off. If his brother could handle Hitler Youth camp as a secret Jew then maybe he too could be courageous enough to try and embrace his new reality.

Two

New Jersey 1965

It was early June, and only two weeks were left at Wayne Valley High. Freddy and Bobby, identical twins, were sitting in math class, looking forward to the end of freshman year and the summer ahead. For the past five summers, they had gone to Camp Ohiwa in the Poconos for eight weeks. These were by far the best eight weeks of their life. Each year, their parents would bring them to camp at the end of June. They would hug their mom and dad goodbye and then unpack in their bunks. Each bunk had twelve beds, six lined up on each side of the room. Between each bed were four shelves that were used to keep clothes and sports equipment and a laundry bag made of netting material. In the back of the bunk were three toilets and two showers. Mostly, they had been with the same boys in their bunk for the past few years. The twins were always popular. They were tall and thin with a mop of brown hair that would constantly fall forward over their eyes. They looked almost identical except for the color of their eyes. Freddy had brown eyes, while Bobby's were green. They were athletic and excelled in all sports, including baseball, basketball, swimming, and soccer. While Freddy may have been brighter and quieter, Bobby was charismatic, charming, and very funny.

Camp had been a coming of age for them, at least for Bobby. At fourteen years old, their hormones were beginning to rage. This was true for all the boys. Jonathan, a good-looking kid with a mole on his cheek, snuck in some of his father's *Playboys*. He would let the other boys look at the magazines in exchange for the camp's most valuable commodity: cans of Coke. You could trade a can of Coke for almost any favor or item you wanted.

One evening, the boys were sitting around the bunk when he brought out his collection. The twins anteed up the two cans of Coke for their chance to look through the magazines. With the magazine opened to the centerfold, Bobby was stunned. There was Peggy Deloach with her large breasts. Her stomach was well-toned, and her skin was tan. And there was a strip of hair running down between her legs. He was surprised to see how big her nipples were. The boys had never seen a naked woman before. Bobby could feel his member spring to action. Harris, noticing Bobby's response, threw a water balloon he was playing with, soaking Bobby's pants. "Fuck off!" said Bobby.

"No one wants to see your boner," laughed Harris. All the boys joined in as Bobby, who had turned bright red, adjusted himself.

"I'm surprised you can even see it," said Freddy. "Where's your magnifying glass?"

"I wouldn't talk, Freddy," said Jonathan. "I'm sure yours is identically tiny."

"We're not identical where it counts," countered Freddy. "You can even ask Roz from last summer. She said it's huge."

"You're such a fucking liar," said Bobby. "The only girl who's ever seen it was Mom when she changed your diapers."

Just then, Jonathan stood up and declared, "Attention, please, everybody freeze! *Dun dun dun dun dun dun da*," and farted loudly.

"Doorknob!" shouted Freddy.

All the boys got up and started punching Jonathan in the arm.

"Kicks, Trix, Chex, Life, Oats!" screamed Jonathan, and all of the boys backed off.

The bunk rule on farting was that when someone farted, another boy would call "doorknob." All of the other boys were then compelled to punch the farter until he either touched a doorknob or shouted the names of five kinds of cereal. The farter was also safe if he yelled "safety" before someone else called "doorknob."

There were no hard feelings. Just the usual banter between boys who lived, slept, ate, and played together each summer at Camp Ohiwa.

Later in the summer, at one of the camp socials, two pretty girls of the same age asked the boys if they wanted to play in the tree house. Jessica, drawn to Bobby's green eyes, took him by the hand, and they climbed the netting to this extraordinary rest area high above the trees. Her friend, Dawn, and Freddy returned to the mess hall to make ice cream sundaes. Bobby could recall every moment of that night. With her light brown hair and thin build, Jessica climbed ahead of him. She had a sweet smell, probably the shampoo in her hair. Bobby became self-conscious for the first time in his life; when she wasn't looking, he sniffed his armpits and pulled back in horror at the onion smell. He hoped his breath was fresh, but he doubted it. The boys had just eaten beef jerky, and he could still taste it. When he sat next to her, he could see the curve of her breast beneath her white shirt and wondered if she looked like the girl from *Playboy*.

"Bobby, have you ever kissed a girl?"

"Yeah, of course. All the time," he lied.

"Oh, well, I've never kissed a boy before. I think you're very handsome."

"Jessica…" He was going to admit his lie, but before he knew it, she moved closer and started to kiss him. He was taken aback by the feeling of her tongue pushing into his mouth, but he quickly recovered and reciprocated. She pulled his hand to feel her breast over her shirt. Mortified by the obvious bulge in his shorts, he took his hand down and covered himself. She looked down and blushed. "Don't worry. I think that's supposed to happen." They kissed some more before coming down from the netting high above the trees.

"Bobby! Bobby!"

He was drawn back from daydreaming as Mr. Stone, his math teacher, stood over him.

"Yes, sir?"

"Well, how do you solve the equation? Go to the board and show the class."

Three

Berlin 1938

The bell rang. It was the last day of tenth grade. David, Eric, and Emma grabbed their backpacks and ran to the corner of Hauptstrasse. David had known Emma and Eric since preschool. The three of them had been best friends for as long as they could remember. "Hold on a second," said Eric. "I'll be right back." He ran to the corner deli while David and Emma stood by. It was a warm June day. The streets were busy. Soldiers in brown uniforms walked up and down the road. Although the soldiers had never bothered David and Emma before, they always got a little anxious and tried avoiding eye contact. It wasn't uncommon for the soldiers to stop the children occasionally. They would ask to see their papers and demand to know what they were doing. But for most Christian children, there usually wasn't any trouble. Eric came out of the store and joined them. "Come on. Let's go."

The three ran along the streets toward the Britzer Garten and then down by the lake. They settled below the shade of a large tree in a secluded area. Eric handed David and Emma a beer.

"To us three!" he said. "David, you are my first cousin and my best friend."

"You know I love you like a brother," David replied.

"And you, Emma, have been like a sister to us both. I'm so excited for the summer. Next week we get on the train, and then six weeks in Bavaria at the Hitler Youth camp."

"Heil Hitler!" David shouted, and Eric returned with the same salute.

"Oh, it's going to be terrible," said Emma. "I'm dreading this summer. I don't know what I would do if it weren't for you both."

"But why are you dreading it, Emma?" David wondered. She stood up and stretched. Both boys stared at her. She did not look like the sweet girl they'd grown up with, but she appeared more beautiful. She had long blonde hair with pale white skin. Her lips were full, and they couldn't help but smile back at her even when she was frowning.

"I don't think it's fair what's going on. Have you seen the new race laws? I heard Jacob and his family are not returning to school next year. His father was fired from his job. He was one of the top professors at the school. Everyone loved him. But they said as he was Jewish, he could no longer teach. And poor Esther's father was arrested last week. We have known Mr. Shanowitz since we were in preschool together. I remember he used to dress up in that ape costume at our birthday parties. He is the kindest and gentlest man I know. But they arrested him for some trumped-up charges. Now Esther, her mom, and her sister have been taken away to live in a re-settlement camp."

"I've heard that the resettlement camps are not pleasant

places and that the people there starve, and some even die," added David.

"But who cares about those filthy Jews?" Eric retorted. "You know they're responsible for all the corruption and disease. Be careful, Emma. You shouldn't talk like that. You never know who might hear you."

"Eric, how can you say that? You don't actually believe that nonsense?" asked Emma.

"Of course I do. It's true."

David involuntarily shuddered, thinking about his secret. Of course, he did not think of himself as a Jew. But his father was born Jewish, and he was secretly Bar Mitzvah'd three years ago. He wondered if Eric's father, Barron, thought as he did, especially as he knew their secret. He was there, for Christ's sake!

"What's wrong, David?" asked Eric. "David?"

"Oh, sorry," he said. "You know I hate politics. Let's go for a swim."

They downed their beers and ran down the bank toward the lake. David and Eric stripped to their underwear and jumped into the cold water. "You coming, Emma?" shouted David. She shook her head. She had always gone swimming with them before, but as she got older, she began to feel more self-conscious. She sat on the side of the bank and watched the boys. They were sixteen now and had grown so handsome. David, with his brown hair, was a couple of inches shorter than Eric, who had short, neat blond hair combed to the side. Both were lean and muscular. She laughed to herself as they wrestled in the water. "Come in!" they cried. Eventually, they climbed out of the water and came to sit with her by the tree.

"I'm sorry about what I said, Emma," Eric continued. "I just get wrapped up in the hype. The Führer's speeches are so inspiring. But in truth, I do feel bad for Esther, Mr. Shanowitz, and of course Jacob and his family."

"Another?" David suggested, trying to change the subject. *Pop.* They opened and downed another bottle.

"Who's in the mood for some truth or dare?" asked Emma, feeling more daring, having had two beers in the hot sun.

"Truth," David said.

"Dare," Eric said in unison.

"Okay, David, you first," she said. "Tell us your biggest secret!"

He couldn't possibly say his biggest secret. "I don't know. I don't have any. Besides, you know all of my secrets."

"You're boring!" she said, feigning a yawn. "Okay, Eric the brave, you asked for a dare."

"Anything you want," he said with arrogance, opening his arms wide. He opened a third beer and passed around another for David and Emma. They clinked bottles. "*Prost!*"

"Eric, you daredevil, strip and run back into the lake while hopping on one leg."

He paused for a second, considering the dare. Then he stood up, looked them both in the eye, and winked. And to their amazement, he dropped his shorts on the ground right in front of them. Emma gasped. She couldn't believe that he would actually do it. He stood motionless and completely exposed for what seemed like an eternity, then turned and hopped into the river.

Once the shock wore off, Emma turned and nodded to the lake, silently asking if they should join. After seeing Eric naked, David felt shy and was afraid that Emma would think less of him. He was not as physically impressive unclothed. He shook his head.

"Come on," she said, smiling at him and pulling him by the arm. With the beer coursing through his veins, he became less shy and stood up. They raced down to the lake, throwing their clothes on the side. David turned just in time to see Emma jumping in. He had never seen a naked girl before, but right then, he knew he was in love with her. They splashed around in the river for hours until sunset. They were three innocent teenage friends whose lives were about to change forever.

Four

Camp Ohiwa, Poconos 1965

As the station wagon rolled along Route 10 West, Bobby and Freddy sat in the back playing thumb wars to kill time. When that got old, they played rock, paper, scissors for a time and then just stared out the window dreaming of the fun to come. At fifteen, they would be the oldest campers this year. If they decided to stay on another year, they would return as counselors-in-training.

"Hey, Dad," Bobby said. "Did you ever go to camp?"

David thought about his other life. Yes, he had been to camp. Hitler Youth camp. And that other camp. His hand inadvertently ran down the length of his left arm, which he always kept covered. He never talked about his former life during the war. His boys had never even seen the numbers crudely tattooed into his arm. He had never told them any-thing about his life in Germany or of his cousin Eric, his brother, or the rest of his family. He never mentioned Emma either. Where were they? What had become of them?

"No, Bobby. I never had the chance to go to camp. As you know, I spent the war hiding in Switzerland. There was no time or money for camps back then. I don't like to talk about that time. Who's thirsty? Honey, why don't you pass back some root beers and cookies for the boys."

As the car continued ahead, Bobby's thoughts turned to Jessica. Bobby and Jessica had stayed in touch for much of the year, writing letters every other month. In their letters, they never mentioned the night at the top of the tree house. Topics were more mundane, like family and school gossip. Jessica lived with her parents in South Jersey outside of Philadelphia. Her father was a dentist, and her mother ran the sisterhood program at the local Jewish temple.

Freddy had not thought about Dawn but was more interested in the Grand Ohiwan he had the chance to do this year. At fifteen years old, the campers could do a three-day excursion in the woods. They would ride bicycles through the mountains one day, hike the next, and rock climb on the final day. Each night they would camp by the fire in tents. This was set to happen about halfway through the eight-week session. When they returned, the children who successfully completed the three-day adventure would get a trophy and an all-you-can-eat ice cream party. But for the boys who had done it before, it was a rite of passage. You left as a child and returned as a man.

"Are you sure you want to do that woods trip?" Mom asked.

"Mom, we talked about this," Freddy replied.

"I know, but I'm nervous about you being out in the woods sleeping in nature. What about bears? David? I heard there are bears in the Poconos."

"Ally, I'm sure the camp will have adequate supervision. And the bears don't usually interact with people. If you come across one, make sure to make a lot of noise. I put a fog horn in your bag. Just stand tall and blow that horn. I'm sure the bears won't bother you."

"Mom, there are no bears in the Poconos. Besides, even if there were any, they wouldn't be Grizzlies or Polar bears."

"Well, just be careful. It makes me so nervous. How will you brush your teeth and go to the bathroom in the woods anyway? I wouldn't want to be around you kids by day three. Pew," she said, holding her nose.

"Mom!" Freddy said, now turning a bright shade of red. "We're going to bring toothbrushes in our overnight bags. If I have to pee, I will just pee on a tree."

"Boys are so lucky," Mom said. "But what will you do if you have to, you know, poop?"

This drew Bobby out of daydreaming as like most boys he loved to joke about farts and poop. "He will dig a hole, squat, and poop in the hole."

"And what? I suppose you use leaves to wipe your tushie?" asked Mom.

"Just make sure it isn't poison ivy," Dad chimed in. "You know what they say about people who go to bed with itchy butts? They wake up with stinky fingers!"

Bobby, Freddy, and their father were all laughing. A moment later, Bobby broke out in laughter again.

"I can't get that thought out of my mind of Freddy squatting in the woods with his bare pimply butt sticking out!" said Bobby, snorting.

"Shut up!" said Freddy, punching Bobby in the arm. "You have pimples on your ass, too."

"Boys, language!" said their father.

"Oh, I don't know, maybe you should just hold it in. That's what I would do," said Mom. "You know what, David, why don't you stop at the convenience store and buy baby wipes and some toilet paper for him to take just in case he can't hold it in. I'm sure the leaves won't clean you very well. You probably shouldn't wear white underwear, just in case."

"I'll be fine," said Freddy, whose face slowly lost the red color of his embarrassment as he turned and looked out the window.

They turned off Route 10, which Dad seemed to miss every year, and continued down the narrow dirt road with tall trees lining either side. They drove underneath the large white sign —Camp Ohiwa, established 1953. The assistant camp director Sheryl was there with a clipboard giving the assignments.

"Hello, boys!" she said through the car window. "Hello Mr. and Mrs. Grossbaum. Welcome back! You will be in Bunk Two this year. That's right, up that road on the right. Once you get settled in, we will be having an all-camp assembly with a pizza dinner and ice cream to follow. The pool and the lake are open if you have time before assembly. We are thrilled to have a new camp director who is very excited and has great new ideas and programs for you kids. Okay, now go on ahead. Jonathan and Justin are already there. They checked in about an hour ago."

David pulled ahead and parked in front of the cabin. There were two counselors sitting on the porch. They stood up and came over to the car to greet the boys.

"Hi. I'm Seth."

"And I'm Adam. Are you guys excited for a great summer?"

Seth and Adam looked like they were about seventeen or

eighteen. They seemed more like older brothers than counselors. Seth was of average height and had brown curly hair. Adam was a few inches taller, muscular, and had straight blond hair. Both were wearing blue t-shirts with *Camp Ohiwa* written across the chest in script lettering.

David had taken the suitcases from the car and was now putting them near the entrance to the bunk. He came over and gave each of his boys a hug.

"Have a great time! I love you guys. See you in eight weeks."

He held back tears. It was always so hard to let go and let someone else be responsible for his boys. He had promised himself years ago that he would never let his loved ones out of his sight or his protection. But over the years, his wife had talked him into sending the boys to sleepaway camp. She felt it was good for them to learn responsibility by being away each summer. While David had a hard time with it, he reasoned that they were at a safe camp with responsible adults, and this was America, after all. It was the complete opposite of his upbringing in Nazi Germany.

Ally turned to her boys, embracing them tightly, tears rolling down her cheeks. "I love you, Freddy. Love you, Bobby. Be good boys and look out for one another."

"Don't worry, Mrs. Grossbaum, we will take good care of your boys," said Adam as he flashed a smile.

"Yes, I'm sure you will. Make sure they eat well and brush their teeth twice a day," she said.

"Mom!" the boys screamed in unison, the embarrassment evident by the flush on their cheeks. "Bye, Mom, bye, Dad," they shouted as they bounded up the steps into their bunk.

Five

Hitler Youth Camp 1938

By the summer of 1938, nearly eighty percent of German children between the ages of ten and eighteen were officially part of the Hitler Youth. The boys and girls in training were kept away from school, church, and their parents to help indoctrinate nearly the entire future population into Hitler's ideologies. The boys were trained initially in song, national pride, and sports. As they progressed in their training, the focus turned to weapons, military functions, and the persecution of non-Aryan Germans, particularly Jews. The girls were trained to cook, clean, keep a good household, and remain fit to be fertile mothers for the next generation of Hitler's youth.

That summer, which had started with skinny dipping in the lake, the three friends were assigned to a camp in Bavaria. Even though Emma was going to the girls' camp, they would all share the same campus and would be able to socialize in the evenings. They rode the train for the five-hour journey from Berlin. There was a cheerful mood on the train. Athletic and beautiful children dressed proudly in their Hitler Youth uniforms sat thinking about the wonderful summer to come.

They could dedicate their time and studies to growing strong for the fatherland. They would be away from their parents' prying eyes, who were generally not as excited about the values being taught. Of course, none of the adults would talk about their opposition to what was being taught by the Hitler Youth. Children were encouraged to spy on their parents, priests, and teachers and report suspicious activities or even anti-Hitler and anti-Nazi rhetoric. It was becoming increasingly common for people to be rounded up at night and sent to concentration camps on account of their oppositional political views. Those sent to camps never returned, and all of their property was confiscated by the Reich.

Once the train reached its destination, the children were loaded onto large transport trucks and driven to the Hitler Youth camps. When they arrived, David, Eric, and Emma got off the truck and wandered through the gate to line up—boys on the left and girls on the right. "See you this evening," said Emma as the boys smiled and waved her off.

"David, there's something I need to tell you."

"Uh-oh, Eric, that sounds ominous."

"Well, I didn't tell you because I wasn't sure what was happening, but do you remember that day in the lake when we, um..."

"How could I forget?"

"Well, a few days later, Emma's parents asked my parents to come over for lunch after church. We all went back to her house. You know our parents have always been terrific friends. It was like any normal day. We all sat around having boring conversations, mostly about the weather, when there was a loud knock at the door. Emma's mom went to answer, and it was Mr. Weber, one of our neighbors. Well, apparently, his wife, who was about nine months pregnant, fell down the stairs and was unconscious and bleeding from a wound on her head, but also it seemed the baby might be coming. He was crying and frantic and wasn't making much sense. Of course, with Emma's father being a doctor and her mother a midwife, they sprang into action. My parents were probably more interested in the excitement than helping, but they jumped up and offered to go as well."

"Why didn't he just take her to the hospital?" David asked.

"Because he's a Jew, obviously, and of course they're not allowed to go to the hospital. I was actually about to ask them why they would even bother helping a filthy Jew, but I remember how that talk upset Emma, so I held my tongue."

"Did you guys go to help as well?"

"No. Her parents told us to stay at the house and clean the kitchen, and that hopefully they would be back in a few hours," Eric replied. "So that's what we did. It only took us a few minutes to clean the kitchen. Emma asked me what I wanted to do, and I just shrugged. You know, ever since seeing her naked by the lake, I couldn't get that image out of my mind. I thought about her all the time. So much so that I found it hard to concentrate on anything but making her mine."

"Eric, I feel the same way. She was so beautiful, like an angel. I think about her all the time, especially when I'm alone."

Eric looked David fiercely in the eyes. They were silent for a few moments. Eric thought back on the rest of the afternoon. He'd told her how much he was in love with her, and she had admitted that she felt the same way about him. They began to kiss in the kitchen. Slow at first and then more passionately. He touched her body all over, feeling her gentle curves and smooth skin. They moved upstairs to Emma's room. He thought they were about to, well, you know. But she stopped him.

"Eric, wait!"

"What's wrong, Emma?"

"I can't. I can't. I'm sorry," she said as tears streamed down her cheeks. "I want to so badly, but we should wait."

He was frustrated, tried again, but again Emma stopped him.

"Eric, stop!"

Ignoring her, he must have pinned her down in the heat of the moment.

"Eric, stop! Please!" she shouted as her hand slipped out and slapped him across the face.

Getting hit snapped him out of the momentary passion. He released her. "Emma, I'm...I'm sorry. I got caught up in the moment."

"I know, I want to do it too, but..."

"It's okay, Emma."

He lay down next to her, sweating from the exertion.

"Eric, put your head back. Let me try another way." She reached over and began to explore his body while they kissed again.

Later, while lying in each other's arms, she said, "Eric. I like you. I want to be with you, and I want you to be my first. But please be patient."

Feeling relieved after the events, he looked back at her and said, "I love you too, Emma."

"What will we tell David?" Emma asked.

She had always known that she liked both of them. They were her best friends, but also, she was so attracted to them in different ways. For Eric, it was more about his pure beauty. While David was also very handsome, he did not match Eric in this category. But with David, she always felt more comfortable. He was sweeter and more sincere. But maybe more like a brother than a boyfriend.

"Don't worry. I will tell my cousin when the time is right. When we are alone," said Eric.

"I hope it doesn't ruin our friendship," said Emma.

"Nothing can ruin our friendship. We will be as close as ever."

"Eric, what's wrong?" said David now, bringing him back to the present.

Eric's cold eyes returned to his cousin. "David, I love you like a brother, but if you ever talk about her like that again, I will kill you."

They stared at each other, Eric cold as ice. David was shocked that his best friend would talk to him like that.

After a few moments, Eric continued, "You see, what I've been trying to tell you is that Emma is now my girlfriend, and I love her very much."

David never realized how much he was also in love with Emma until hearing these words drained the blood from his face. He felt dizzy and nauseous, similar to his thirteenth birthday when his parents informed him that he was a Jew.

They didn't talk while waiting in line to check in at the camp. Eventually, they reached the front.

"Name?" said an official sitting at the desk with two SS officers behind him.

"Eric Ba— "

"Is that how you salute me, son?" the official barked at him.

"Sorry, sir! Heil Hitler," Eric and David shouted in unison, clicking their heels together and raising their right hands.

"Heil Hitler," the official responded. "That's better. Now your names, please?"

"Eric Bauer, sir."

"David Wagner, sir."

"My name is Herr Baldur Benedikt von Schirach, and I oversee the Hitler Youth."

Schirach was a thirty-one-year-old man with an oval face and the slightest of double chins. In 1931 Adolf Hitler assigned him to be in charge of the entire Hitler Youth, whose membership had grown to over 1,000,000 children. Hitler tasked him to teach these children to become committed Nazis and train them for war and life in post-war Germany.

"Hmm. David? Sounds like a Jewish name. Let me see your paperwork."

"No, sir, I'm not a Jew!" David hissed, handing his papers to the official.

"He's no filthy Jew," said Eric. "He's my cousin."

"Well, maybe you are a Jew too. Let me see your papers."

He studied David and Eric's documents, then handed them to the SS officer behind him, who studied them and looked at the boys very carefully. The other children in the boys' and girls' lines were watching. The SS officers from the girls' lines now came over and surrounded the boys.

"The papers look in order," said the SS officer. "They can pass to the medical tent."

"Not so fast," said Schirach.

David was beginning to sweat profusely, while Eric stood calmly at attention.

"David, why is your face red? Your shirt is soaked. What are you hiding?" asked the official. "You know, the more I look at you with that nose of yours, there is something about its shape. It doesn't look Jewish, but it's not quite right either."

"Sir, I promise you I am not Jewish. Please, my papers prove it. I can recite Christian prayers for you. Our father who art in heaven, hallowed be thy name..."

"Any monkey can be taught to say that!" interrupted Schirach. "Gentlemen, lower your pants. We will see if you have been circumcised."

"Here?" asked David, alarmed at all the boys and girls in line staring at them.

"Now!" shouted Herr Schirach as one of the SS soldiers unholstered his gun and began to raise it.

The boys immediately loosened their belts and dropped their pants and underwear to the ground, very much aware of all the eyes on them. Some of the girls in the adjacent line began to giggle. David did all he could not to let go of his bladder under the intense inspection. Eric, though surely embarrassed, kept his head up and shoulders back.

Schirach grunted, apparently satisfied that they were both uncircumcised. "You may dress now. You can never be too careful. Jews are very sneaky and can hide in our very ranks. I trust you will enjoy your time here. You may go to the medical tent for inspection and then off to your cabins. Tonight will be very exciting for you both, I trust."

"Heil Hitler," they shouted and hurried away.

Emma moved through the line and was sent into the girls' medical tent, where she was asked to remove her clothes, except for her undergarments, and stand in line. Several nurses in white uniforms were there assisting the doctor who assessed the girls. The tent smelled of perspiration. There were several stations. Each girl was weighed on the scale first, and then her height was taken. Emma stepped on the scale.

"Weight 53.6 kilograms, height 165 centimeters!" the nurse announced. "You may move to the next station." There were two more girls in Emma's group, Beverly and Gertrude. Beverly stepped up to the scale first, and her height and weight were also found to be satisfactory.

"Next!" said the nurse, frowning at Gertrude. "Come on. Step up!" Gertrude, a portly girl, hesitantly stepped on the scale.

"Weight 81 kilograms, height 157.4 centimeters. Please wait here for the doctor."

Dr. Virchow came in and reviewed the data. "Name, please."

"Gertrude, sir."

"Gertrude...that's a pretty name. How did a girl with such a pretty name end up so fat? Judging by your height and weight, it appears that you spend most of your time eating donuts and cake and no time exercising. It is disgusting and unhealthy for a girl of sixteen to be so fat. What kind of man would want you for a wife? Do you have no shame? Didn't your mother teach you?"

Tears were now streaming down Gertrude's face. "Please, sir, my mother and father are both, well, heavy, so I cannot help it."

"Your parents being fat, lazy slobs is no excuse for you. What do you think the Führer would say if he saw you? But don't worry. We will fix you. During the eight-week session, you and the other piglets must join the extra workouts beginning at four thirty a.m. before your regular activities. In addition, you will be restricted to half portions until your weight falls below fifty-eight kilograms. Failure to achieve this goal will have dire consequences. Understood?"

"Yes, sir," uttered Gertrude.

"Dismissed!"

Emma reached out to comfort Gertrude as the group moved toward the next station and was sharply reprimanded.

"There will be no comfort given to the pig. Move on to the next station," said the doctor.

The rest of the examinations were not quite so remarkable. The doctors and nurses took records and measured everything one could think of measuring, from eyesight down to the angle of the curve of the fingernails. Finally, they were sent to their assigned cabins to get settled in.

Each day after dinner, the boys and girls were allowed to socialize until nine p.m., at which point they were to return to their cabins where they would brush their teeth, wash their face, and then lights out.

Later that evening, Emma met up with David and Eric.

"Oh, I'm so happy to see you!" exclaimed Emma as she ran up to them.

They were walking from the mess hall toward the central

common area. This was a field with trees, benches, and picnic tables surrounded by the girls' cabins on one side and the boys' cabins on the other. Most of the children in this section of the camp were older teenagers. The camp was a gorgeous expanse of grassy fields, small streams, a lake, and various camp buildings. The Bavarian Alps could be seen in the distance.

"How was your medical exam?" Eric asked.

"Passed with flying colors, but what else would you expect from me?" She winked.

"Well, you always did get straight A's in everything," said David.

"I imagine it went a little better than yours. I was so frightened when Schirach was questioning you."

"You saw that?" asked David as his face burned red.

"Oh, don't worry, it's not like I haven't seen it before," she teased. "But I imagine it was the first time for the other twenty or so girls waiting in line. But I thought you were both so brave. I would have peed my pants for sure."

"I think we almost did," said Eric. "Of course, it wouldn't have mattered as we were not wearing pants anyway."

They all started to laugh. It was nice to be together again. The three of them all felt a sense of comfort in the familiarity. "Would you guys like some water? They have drinks and strudel. I'll go get some," said Eric.

Both said yes.

When they were alone for the first time, David and Emma looked at each other. They started to talk at the same time and stopped. "You first, Emma," said David.

"David, I wanted to tell you something. We have all been very good friends for so long. But something's happened—"

"Yes, I know," interrupted David. "Eric told me that you are his girlfriend now."

"Well, I just don't want you to be upset because I love you both. But now I'm going to give my heart to Eric."

"Emma, there is no need to explain. It's fine. I'm happy for both of you. I love you both, too, and I couldn't think of two better people to be together."

Emma looked away. She was relieved that David wasn't upset, but at the same time, she felt hurt that he wasn't. Strangely she loved them equally and couldn't say which one more. But it was as if he didn't even care.

"Well, that makes me feel better now," announced Emma.

Eric returned with the water and strudels. When the horn sounded, it meant it was time to return to the cabins for the evening. "David, I'll catch up to you in a moment," said Eric.

As David returned to the bunk, he turned a moment, looking for Eric, and saw them kissing. It was a long and passionate kiss. He couldn't help but stare at them, longing to be in Eric's place.

Then a bugle sounded, summoning the children to return to the main auditorium. David caught up with Emma and Eric as they entered the building. They found some seats toward the front of the hall along the right side as children filed in and filled the rows. There were two pillars about ten feet apart on the stage. Chained to each pillar was a person with a black bag over their head. Their arms were tied behind their backs, and their legs were shackled to the pillars. In the center of the stage was a podium. Large red Nazi banners were hanging on either side of the stage and along the walls on either side of the auditorium. A large poster of the Führer was hanging from the ceiling over the center of the stage above the podium.

The children looked at each other excitedly, wondering what would happen. The room was noisy with chatter.

"I wonder what this is about?" asked Emma. "Who are those two people with bags over their heads?"

"I heard they have some entertainment here every night," said a girl next to her. "My older sister was here last year and said they had a different nightly surprise."

"I wonder if the Führer will be here," wondered a boy in the row ahead of them.

The crowd settled down as Baldur Benedikt von Schirach walked onto the stage, followed by four SS officers who took their places, two on either side of him.

"Settle down! Silence!" he shouted, and the children grew silent.

"Please, everyone, sit down. I have been charged by Adolf Hitler himself to teach you everything you need to know. First, I am so proud of you all for being here. Our Führer has been hard at work restoring Germany as the number one country in the world. He is trying to establish the Third Reich, which will rule the earth for a thousand years. But he cannot do it alone. We need each and every one of you to do your part. You are on the right track to joining our group.

"This summer, you will train hard to become faster, stronger, and smarter than your enemies. You will have daily physical exercise. You will learn to use weapons. You will learn to use your fists. I don't expect you all to make it to the end of this session. There is no place in the Third Reich for weakness. Those of you who cannot be made hard and strong will be eliminated. I don't expect you to be perfect today, but by the end of the summer, you will be ready for anything the Führer may ask of you.

"In addition to your muscles, you will also sharpen your mind. To beat our enemies, we need to be smarter than them. We have enemies everywhere. We have enemies abroad, but more dangerously, we have enemies at home. Our enemies are intelligent and cunning. It will take all of your training to defeat them. For Germany to survive, we must identify and rid ourselves of the weak, the infirm, the disabled, and most importantly, the Jews. The Jews have spent years infiltrating our way of life. They can be found in government, law enforcement, education, banking, and every business we know. They have a network that looks to control our society. Our Führer has worked hard to find and eliminate them from these positions. But as I said, they are cunning, and many have escaped our detection. To that end, today we have caught a Jew trying to blend in and train amongst our ranks. Our doctors discovered him during examinations today, and upon further questioning, he has admitted that he is a Jew. Remove his hood."

An SS officer stepped forward and removed the bag from the first boy tied to the pillar. "This is Raul Von Reck, but his real name is Levy Schwartz." The boy stood there with his hands tied behind his back. He looked to be about fourteen. He had brown curly hair and was of average build and height. His face was red, and he had bruises along his left eye. His face was dirty where tears had flowed.

"The other boy tied to a pole is not a Jew. But he's almost as bad. His name is Arnold Strauss. Arnold is fourteen years old. He knew that Levy was a Jew and lied to the SS officers, trying to protect the filthy Jew. After a little persuasion, he came clean."

The SS officers removed his hood, revealing a frightened boy with blond hair and blue eyes. He was tall and thin. His face was swollen, and he had dried blood along the side of his face, neck, and shirt. He also looked as if he had been crying.

"Where are David Wagner and Eric Bauer?"

David felt faint at the mention of his name. Had they found out about him as well? His shirt instantly became soaked with sweat. Emma squeezed his hand.

"We are here, sir," Eric called out.

"Ah, yes. Would the two of you please join me on the stage?"

They made their way down the aisle and up onto the stage. Eric, who was holding it together better than David, pushed him along. "Come on, David," he whispered. "It will be okay. We have nothing to hide."

"Earlier today," Schirach continued, "I mistook David and Eric for Jews. I humiliated them, making them take their pants off in front of many of you boys and girls. I was wrong. Neither of these boys are Jewish. They are good, strong young men who will hopefully have excellent careers within the Reich. To make amends for their earlier disgrace, I thought to reward them by allowing them to punish these two criminals."

Eric smiled, clearly happy with the turn of events. David could not believe what he was being asked to do. These two boys tied to the pillars could easily have been him and Eric. They did nothing wrong other than being Jewish or a friend of a Jew. They were no different than they were, except that Eric did not know David was secretly half-Jewish.

"Here." He handed each boy a whip. "I want each of you to give Arnold ten lashes."

The SS guards turned Arnold around and secured him to the pole, ripping his shirt off. "Harboring a Jew will not be tolerated. Eric, begin!"

Eric went first. His whip lashed down across Arnold's back. A loud shriek filled the auditorium. "Again," said Schirach. "Harder, harder!" Eric's whip came down over and over again. Arnold screamed and cried as blood flowed down his back from the repeated lacerations. With each crack of the whip, Eric began to enjoy it more and more. He actually began to smile.

"Okay, that's ten. David, your turn," said Schirach.

David raised his hand and cracked the whip down on Arnold's back. The boy screamed in pain. With each crack of the whip, David became more upset to the point tears began to trickle down his face.

"I know it is difficult to punish a fellow German. Especially a beautiful German boy like Arnold, but he has committed a terrible crime. You will learn that we cannot trust Germans who protect Jews. They are almost as bad."

When the ten lashes were complete, the boys handed the whips back to Schirach. Arnold was lying there on the floor. His back was bloodied, and his arms and legs were still tied to the pillar. He was quietly moaning now.

"Arnold will be sent to a work camp where he will do

hard labor until he repents for his crime," said Herr Schirach. "And now we must punish the Jew."

Both boys stared Levy in the eyes. He seemed so young. He was trembling now, tears running down both cheeks.

Schirach unholstered his gun. "Who will do the honors?"

Eric's and David's eyes opened wide, looking at the gun. They looked at each other as the silence filled the room. David's heart was pounding so hard he was sure Schirach could hear it.

"I will, sir," said Eric, taking the gun from Schirach.

Levy began to sob, now begging for his life.

"Please, sir, I'm sorry. I'm sorry."

"Eric, kill the animal," commanded Schirach.

What is going on? He's not really going to do this, is he? thought David.

Eric raised the gun and pointed it at the child. Levy lost control of his bladder and soaked his pants.

"Disgusting animals," said Schirach. "Okay, that's enough talk. Do it!"

"Shemah Yisrael," were the last words David heard Levy utter.

With that, Eric pulled the trigger. *Bang*, and then silence. Levy's body fell to the floor, making a thud, his legs twitching for a moment before becoming completely still. The auditorium fell silent.

"Well done, Eric. You have made the Reich proud. You two can go back to your seats. No one should feel bad. The animal was an enemy who tried to infiltrate our camp. All we did today was rid ourselves of another enemy. On my command, you may all get up and return to your cabins. We have a busy day ahead of us tomorrow. Dismissed."

Turning to his SS officers, he said, "Have Arnold take the body to the truck outside and then have him clean up this blood and piss. Disgusting Jews."

Six

Camp Ohiwa 1965

Summer camp started off great with the opening week ice-breaker exercises. For most of the kids, they weren't necessary because they'd been with the same bunkmates for several summers. For Bobby, besides his brother Freddy, he felt like his bunk was full of his brothers. He'd shared many summers with Justin, Jonathan, and Harris. Each morning they would wake up and brush their teeth and then walk across the large central field toward a mess hall where they would eat pancakes, waffles, eggs, or cereal and drink chocolate milk. They usually didn't take showers in the morning but instead in the afternoon after returning from a swim in the lake. Even then, they would try to get out of showering, especially if the counselors were lenient. Both Adam and Seth were pretty cool. Adam spent most of his time flirting with Chery, a counselor from one of the girl's bunks. Seth could be bribed to look the other way with a can of Coke.

Freddy, who was more adventurous than the other boys, was a member of the Ohiwa Bears Club. He was awakened every morning at six a.m., and he would run down and jump into the lake with the other bears and then return in time for the regular wake-up call for the rest of the bunk.

After breakfast, the boys would begin morning activities, which were different every day. The different activities included archery, rifle range, soccer, baseball, basketball, tennis, bicycle riding, arts and crafts, and rock climbing. After the morning activity, they would go to lunch and then on to an afternoon activity. On Monday, Wednesday, and Friday, they had swimming in the pool with lessons and free play. Bobby frequently won the pool tennis ball competition. Here, they would take turns running and jumping off the diving board and catching a tennis ball thrown by pool director Sal. If you dropped the ball, you would be eliminated. On Tuesday and Thursday, they would spend the afternoon by the lake with the girls' bunks. They could just hang out or swim or even go water skiing.

Freddy and Bobby were both athletic and easily picked up water skiing, but neither one was as graceful as Jessica. It was in the first week of camp down by the lake that Bobby saw her for the first time. Her boat came into the dock, and she got off along with Dawn. She was wearing a navy-blue bathing suit, and her wet hair hung down over the white towel wrapped around her torso. Her long legs were already nicely tanned, and she looked even more beautiful than Bobby remembered. Dawn got off right behind her. She had also grown more beautiful over the summer. Her wet blonde hair with red highlights glistened in the sunshine. She was thin and slightly less tan than Jessica.

They saw the boys hanging out on the beach with their bunkmates and walked over.

"Jessica, hi," was all Bobby could think to say. After all the letters they had written back and forth this year, he was embarrassed that he couldn't think of something wittier.

She smiled. "Hi, Bobby. Hi, Freddy."

"Hi, Dawn. You gals looked terrific out there," said Freddy. "We were just about to go water skiing too. How's the water?"

"It's real cold, but you get used to it quickly," said Dawn. "Freddy, how was your year? You know I wrote to you. Did you get my letter?"

"Really?" said Freddy. "No, I never got it." Freddy felt sudden relief. He had been somewhat envious that Jessica had written Bobby and was upset that Dawn hadn't done the same for him. "Maybe it got lost in the mail?"

"That's okay, you're here now," replied Dawn. "Do you guys want to go water skiing now? We can join you for another turn."

"Sure, let's go," Bobby said with his charming smile.

"Make sure you tie your bathing suits tight, boys," said Harris. "You wouldn't want to embarrass yourself if your trunks should slip off when you fall."

"Well, they can always use the cold water as an excuse," laughed Justin.

"Shut up, dude," responded Freddy.

The girls giggled, too, as they all ran off toward the dock to go water skiing again.

On board the boat, they watched as Freddy went first. He was able to get up on the second try and, after a few moments, actually looked pretty smooth doing it. It was clear that he had also grown since last summer. His chest and arms had become more muscular, and he had the start of a six-pack. They each took turns and then watched as Harris went skiing.

"So, what do you guys think of the new camp director?" asked Jessica.

"We haven't really met him yet except for the first night when he gave the opening address. It seems like he has big plans to change the summer itinerary. Maybe it'll be more fun," said Bobby.

The new man in charge was a far cry from the former camp director, Murray, who had been like another parent away from home. Murray was warm. He would hug the younger children and read them stories, especially when they were homesick.

"I don't know. He scares me a bit. His eyes are cold," said Jessica.

"But he is kind of cute," said Dawn. "He's tall and muscular and has that beautiful blond hair and chiseled face."

"I'm excited to see what he means by the new twist on color wars this year," said Bobby.

Color wars was traditionally the second to last week of camp and was the highlight of the summer. All of the campers were divided into two colors: red and yellow. They would compete in different Olympic-style games during the week, with one team eventually coming out on top. Each night at dinner, the updated tallies would be announced and the daily stars were recognized.

"Freddy, are you still planning on going on the Grand Ohiwan this summer?" asked Dawn. "I was actually thinking about joining this year as well."

"Wow, that would be so fun, but it's only open to boys," responded Freddy.

"No, the new camp director announced that girls could go this year and that he would be there to personally supervise. Jessica might join us as well," said Dawn.

"Well, I'm thinking about it," said Jessica as she smiled at Bobby.

"I guess you've twisted my arm. I'm in too, then," said Bobby as he smiled back at her. "Do you really think you can rough it for three days and two nights in the woods? Don't worry, if nature calls, Freddy came prepared. He can share his baby wipes."

"Ewww!" said the girls.

"You're such an asshole, Bobby," said Freddy, turning bright red as they all broke out into laughter.

*

The weeks leading up to the Grand Ohiwan were filled with fun, sun-soaked days. The campers played sports and performed crafts all day. Each evening was filled with new and fun activities, such as putting on plays, roasting marshmallows by the fire and telling ghost stories, paintball fights, and swimming in the lake under the stars. The relationships that were born last summer continued to develop. Jessica and Bobby, as well as Freddy and Dawn, continued their innocent romance. They would steal a few private moments with each other. Their passion grew, but they never did anything more than kiss despite the boys trying their luck to push it further. The girls always playfully shut them down. There was some touching, but always with clothes on.

A few strange things happened over the early parts of

the summer, and they all involved the new director. On one occasion, Jonathan was caught sneaking into the mess hall and having a donut. He wasn't hungry. It was really just a practical joke. In the past, there was always a little mischief at camp and generally it was dealt with by maybe being forced to miss dessert one night or losing privileges to go to an evening activity. But this time, when Jonathan was caught stealing the donut, he was called into the director's office. When he came back to the bunk two hours later, his eyes were red. Clearly, he had been crying. The twins tried to ask him what the director said, but he wouldn't say. He didn't come to dinner, just stayed in his bed all night. The next day he joined everyone for activities but was still very melancholic. He continued to refuse to talk about it. The next day, after swimming, when the boys got back to the bunk to change for dinner, it was clear what had happened. When Jonathan took off his bathing suit, his butt was covered in welts, some starting to turn black and blue. Harris, seeing this first, said, "Holy shit, Jon, what happened? Your ass is covered in bruises. Did he hit you?"

Jonathan quickly pulled on his boxers and lay down on the bed. With tears coming down his cheeks, he finally told his friends what happened.

"I was invited to sit in the director's office. When I walked in, he was silently staring out the window, not turning to greet me as I came in. Eventually, I sat down. After what seemed like forever, he turned and faced me. He asked if I'd enjoyed the donut, and I laughed, thinking it was a joke. 'What's so funny?' he said. 'Do you think stealing is your right? Do you people never learn?' I was confused, and then he went on about how he'd thought the lessons of years past would teach people like me to live like ordinary decent folk, but that it's clearly in my blood. 'You cannot help it,' he said. 'You're wired to cheat and steal from honest ordinary people.' I asked him what he was talking about, and he said, 'You know what I'm talking about, Jew! Now stand up. At this camp, we will treat all infractions very seriously.'"

"Wait," said Freddy. "He called you a Jew? Who is this guy?"

"There's more," replied Jonathan. "I said to him, 'You're kidding, right?' and he said, 'I'm dead serious, Jonathan. Up! You will learn your place.' Then he walked toward me, lifted me by the collar, and threw me toward the desk."

Jonathan went on to tell them that he yelled "Stop!" and started to cry, totally shocked at what was happening to him, but the director's eyes were cold and soulless. There would be no pleading. Seeing this, Jonathan resigned himself to what was to come and bent over the desk. He screamed with each lash of the belt across his butt.

When it was over, the director came back and put his arm around Jonathan, seemingly remorseful now. His eyes looked wet. "You know, Jonathan, I have been through a lot in my life and have seen terrible things. You know I was at a concentration camp in Germany. Do you know what that means? It was a wicked place, the most difficult time of my life. That is why I took this job as your camp director, so I can help you kids. You will learn the discipline and skills needed to navigate this new world. Do you want my help to change?"

Jonathan, not responding, looked away. He continued, "You know that's why your parents have sent you here under my care, so I can really help you change. Have you met my son, Otto? He is the new head of athletics. He can really help you. You know, he was born during the war. Yes, in 1939. Can you imagine his life as a little boy during the war? But he learned discipline, and he will help you boys."

"May I go now?" asked Jonathan.

"Yes, go get ready for dinner." Jonathan walked toward the door. "Oh, Jonathan," said the director, his cold eyes returning. "I wouldn't go telling your friends about this. This was between me and you, and I would be very disappointed if you shared it. Very."

When Jonathan finished telling them what had happened, shocked silence fell over the group.

"I can't believe it," said Harris. "He really freaking hit you?"

"Did you try to fight back?" asked Bobby.

"Guys, he's really powerful. He picked me up by my shirt collar and practically threw me across the room with one hand."

"Shit, dude. I'm sorry. Did he do anything else to you? You know, besides hit you?" asked Bobby.

"No. He just whipped me with a belt and then lectured me and called me a Jew."

"What the fuck? Did you call your dad?" asked Freddy. "My dad is going to freak out. He moved here from Europe. He was there during the war."

"I tried to call my dad this morning, but the cord to the camp phone was cut. That's the only one besides the one in the camp office. I'm going to write them a letter and mail it today. Guys, this director is insane. One minute there was hate and murder in his eyes, and the next he seemed remorseful, and then back again."

"Let's all write letters to our parents," said Bobby.

*

A couple of days later, while eating breakfast, the director walked in and took a microphone to address the campers.

"Good morning, Camp Ohiwa," he said with a big smile and thick accent. "I trust you have been enjoying the first couple of weeks of camp. For those of you who I have not yet met, my name is Eric and I'm thrilled that your parents have entrusted your care to me. As I mentioned to those I've met, my goal is to make this camp experience even more wonderful than before. I have also decided we need to focus more on your overall wellbeing, which includes enhancing your skills for the future. I don't really like to talk about it, but just twenty years ago, right before you were born, the world was at war. It was incredibly tragic. I saw and endured horrors that you cannot imagine. In today's world, you will need to be strong, honest citizens, and we will start that by making you strong and honest campers. Instead of morning sports, we will have a new curriculum. Each morning we will wake up at six a.m. You will quickly dress, make your bed, and then go for morning exercises, which will include running, climbing, and swimming. After that, you will return to your bunks, where you will brush your teeth and shower. We will then line up for roll call outside your bunks. At roll call, you will stand erect, and when your turn comes, you will shout your name and a number that will be assigned to you. You will see by making these simple changes, you will feel more mentally and physically fit. You will be better prepared for the rest of your day.

"In life, you will face many challenges. There are groups

of dishonest people out there looking to take from you if you are not prepared. I will have you ready to face the world. All I ask from you is that you follow these few rules. I urge you to leave me a note in my mailbox if you notice someone who is not following the rules. It is not snitching but rather keeping everyone honest.

"Other housekeeping matters. I have put in a call to the phone company, but it seems the parts are on backorder, so it will not likely be fixed this summer. If someone knows who committed this prank, please come forward and let me know confidentially. Also, in the interest of full disclosure, I will be reading all outgoing mail to make sure your spelling and grammar are correct. I will give you feedback. I'm sure your English teachers will thank me next year when they see how much you've improved over the summer. I have nothing else for you at this time. Let's go have a great day!"

Seven

Berlin 1938

The Hitler Youth summer camp came to an end in August, and the children returned home for a three-week break before school was to begin again. The camp was transformative for many of the children. No matter their experience leading up to camp, they all came home changed. The eight weeks had hardened them. Not just their muscles but also their minds. The cruel teachings made the children immune to violence. After the first night of camp when Eric was asked to execute the fourteen-year-old Jewish boy, things changed for all of them. They had learned to distance emotion. There was no room for sorrow now. German pride and strength were at the forefront of their minds. Gone was the innocence of childhood, replaced by an almost robotic singular focus. The focus was on the promotion of Nazi ideologies and the elimination of Nazi enemies. Of course, not all of the children were successfully brainwashed.

Emma had always been a tolerant spirit but came home from camp only slightly committed to the Nazi ideologies. She was fortunate not to have had to participate in any of the violence. For the most part, this was reserved for the male youth. But she was witness to the barbarity of it.

David kept his secret at camp. He also managed to avoid having to commit violence except for the first night when he whipped Arnold. He was horrified at what he had done. He remembered seeing the deep lacerations that he helped create on the child's back. But even worse than that, not a day passed when he did not recall the image of Levy. Every night when he went to sleep, he could see Levy's trembling face covered with dirt and tears. He kept hearing the last words that Levy whispered right before Eric pulled the trigger. "Shemah Yisrael." *Bang.* He heard it over and over in his mind. "Shemah Yisrael." *Bang.* "Shemah Yisrael." *Bang.* And then he would see Levy's crumpled body with his eyes open and dead staring right back at him. He had learned that prayer on the day of his Bar Mitzvah but never dared utter it out loud.

He never spoke to Eric about that event. He didn't dare. Sometimes when they were alone, he would quietly talk to Emma, who tried to comfort him. She admired that he kept his humanity even when everyone else seemed to be transforming into good Nazis.

Eric, on the other hand, thrived at camp. His part in the execution that first night made him somewhat of a hero amongst the other children. He excelled at sports, wrestling, weaponry, and classroom studies. He was widely recognized as one of the leading children and was told as much. Near the end of camp, Schirach called him into his office.

"Heil Hitler," shouted Eric.

"Heil Hitler," Schirach responded.

Schirach was sitting behind his desk smoking a cigar. Eric stood at attention.

"Eric, I am very pleased with your progress. I see a strong future for you within the Reich. When the summer is over, and you return home, you will not be returning to school. I have put forward your name, and you will be assigned to the SS. You will train as an SS officer and serve in your hometown of Berlin."

Eric was taken aback. He had never been a straight-A student and never received many compliments beyond his good looks. For the first time in his life, he was not just getting by but excelling. He was a star within the Hitler Youth and was being recognized for it.

Schirach continued, "But I have bigger plans for you than merely joining the SS. As you know, Hitler has many enemies, and it is a physical problem for the Reich. We need a place to house and ultimately dispose of these enemies. We are in the process of setting up many work camps where our enemies will be dealt with. I believe you have the right temperament to excel in this environment. You may even have the opportunity to lead the operations of one of these work camps if your career progresses the way I expect it to. Keep up the good work, son. Dismissed."

Eric told Emma and David of his conversation, and they acted appropriately pleased for him. But in private they were both concerned about how radical he had become. His romance with Emma continued over the summer. They stole away for private moments as often as they could. With his newfound star power and the backing of the commandant, certain liberties were granted to him. The SS officers would turn a blind eye if he and Emma skipped dinner or the evening entertainment in order to get some private time in the cabins. While they would kiss and pleasure each other, Emma never allowed Eric to take her virginity. Despite their passion and longing, Emma was scared of who Eric was becoming. Even at the height of passion, she could never let her guard down completely. While she loved him, she could not understand how he could kill that boy in cold blood. It did not seem to bother him even in the slightest, and this frightened her. Of course, he'd had no choice, but he didn't even hesitate when the opportunity presented itself.

In the meantime, her friendship with David continued to grow. They talked with each other every day. They had shared concerns about Eric and about what was happening to the other Hitler Youth. On the last night of camp, while Eric was busy with a special dinner with the commandant, David and Emma shared some alone time by the fire pit.

Emma began to cry. "What is it, Emma?" David asked as he reached for her hand.

"David, I'm so scared all of the time. I'm scared when I'm alone with Eric."

"Did he hurt you?" asked David.

"No, he is gentle with me, usually. But I'm scared of the person he has become. I mean, I know I shouldn't care because that boy was just a Jew, but still, I do care. It never bothered Eric at all. I think he liked the power he held over that boy and doesn't regret taking his life." The tears streamed down Emma's face. "I mean, that boy had a family. What about his poor mother and father? What about the life and love he will never experience?"

David hugged her, and they gently swayed. She looked up at him. Their eyes met, reflecting the glow of the fire. Emma reached up and kissed David passionately. She felt so safe in his embrace.

"Emma, we better not."

But neither heeded his warning. They continued to kiss, each becoming more passionate. They lay down next to the fire. She unbuttoned her blouse as they continued to kiss. She could sense him becoming more excited as well. In the heat of the moment, she let David do what Eric never had. In just moments, it was over. They lay there, entangled in each other's embrace, panting and alone by the fire.

Eight

Grand Ohiwan 1965

Bobby, Freddy, Jessica, and Dawn said goodbye to their friends. They would be back in three days after the Grand Ohiwan. They got up early that morning and packed their bags according to the list that the camp had given them. Going on the trip would be a total of eight boys and four girls. They would be led by camp director Eric, along with two of the counselors, Adam and Serena. By the time the children arrived at the bus right after breakfast, Eric, Adam, and Serena had already packed away all of the equipment they would need, including the mountain bicycles, canoes, harnesses for climbing, and the tents. Also packed were essential food and extra fresh water supplies for the three-day trip. On the first day, they had a ninety-minute ride to the start of their adventure. The plan was for the bus driver to drop them off along with the bicycles and then meet them at the campground that evening. They were to ride about thirty miles through uneven terrain.

Eric announced, "I'm very proud of you who have volunteered to get back to nature and use nothing but the essential equipment to survive. My plan is to do about sixty percent of the trail and stop for lunch near Lake Opachee. You can eat and then go for a swim. Then we will complete the last twelve miles or so to our campground. I have some surprises in store for you along the way. Good luck, campers!"

And they were off. The first part of the trip was quite comfortable. It wasn't too hot. They had the shade from the trees above and rode in one line. Eric led from the front. Serena, the girls' counselor, was in the middle, and Adam, the boys' counselor, rode at the back to make sure they didn't lose any stragglers. Much of the morning went without incident until, as they were coming down a hill, Dawn squeezed too hard on her front brake and was flung over the front of the handlebars, landing hard on the dirt path. Luckily, she didn't get too hurt. She bruised her forearm and her knee and skinned part of her nose. Serena signaled and the group came to a stop. Freddy was the first one there at her side.

"Oh my God, Dawn, are you okay?" he asked.

"Yeah...I think so."

"Did you hit your head? Your nose is bleeding."

Eric came charging up from the front and quickly took Freddy's place.

"Let me have a look at you," said Eric as he gently caressed her face. He checked her arms and knees with unexpected gentleness. "There, there, you will be perfectly fine. Just a little scratch," he said as he wiped the blood off her nose with a wet towel. "Now stand up if you can and see if it hurts to walk."

Dawn did as she was told and nodded. "I think I'm good."

"We can stop here for lunch if you like and take a rest," suggested Eric.

"It's okay, I can continue."

"Atta girl. Then we're off," he said, smiling at Dawn as they all returned to their bikes.

The last part of the morning ride was more strenuous and mostly uphill. They finally reached the lake around one p.m. Adam and Serena handed out peanut butter and jelly sandwiches and potato chips. The foursome sat together for lunch. Freddy said, "How are you feeling, Dawn?"

"Just a little sore," she replied.

"I was surprised to see how nice and gentle Eric was," said Bobby.

"Yeah, totally different than what Jonathan said about the whipping," said Freddy.

"I think he has split personalities," said Jessica.

"Who wants to go for a swim?" asked Dawn.

The lake was large but not too big that they couldn't see the other side. It was a beautiful July day. The sun was beaming overhead, and the sky was blue with not a single cloud. The water was crystal clear, cool, and inviting. The boys went off in one direction and the girls in another to find some privacy behind the trees to change.

They spent about forty minutes splashing about in the lake with the other children and counselors. The water was so refreshing. Dawn got up on Freddy's shoulders, and Jessica did the same with Bobby. They laughed and played chicken with each other. Eric suddenly blew his whistle and waved for the campers to come in.

"Time to dry off. We need to be off in twenty minutes

so we can make it to the campground before sunset." He was smiling, watching the children walk out of the lake, when he noticed Steven walking out. Steven was a little heavier than the others and seeing him made Eric's mood change.

"Everyone, come here," Eric began. "As I told you earlier, I am very proud of each of you for signing up for this adventure. You knew it wasn't going to be physically easy, but you took a chance. Bobby, step up here for a moment."

"Yes, sir."

"Part of being healthy and organized is taking care of your body," said Eric. "Have a look at Bobby. He is a healthy boy who takes pride in himself. Notice his arms and legs are muscular. His chest is flat, and his belly is tight. You can see his abs have definition. His posture is erect. Now, Steven, come stand here next to Bobby."

Steven walked up, and both boys stood there in just their bathing suits. "Clearly, Steven doesn't take pride in his appearance. When you look at both boys together, you can tell who is lazy and who is not. You can tell who prefers sports and who prefers to eat cake."

Steven's face was turning red. "I'm not lazy. I like to play soccer and baseball and I'm really good," he muttered.

"Silence," shouted Eric. "Now, aside from you and Bobby, there are ten other children here. One at a time, I would like you to point out differences in Steven's and Bobby's body shapes. I believe Steven will find this lesson motivating for him. Jessica, you first. Tell us what you think about Steven's belly."

"I think, I think they're, uh, both normal looking," she said.

"Steven deserves to know the truth so he can improve.

Please give specific thoughts on Steven's and Bobby's belly. If you are unable to provide good feedback, perhaps we will take a turn examining your body," said Eric.

Jessica stood there for a while, frightened of being put in the spotlight but also not wanting to hurt Steven's feelings. She looked at Bobby. His abs were cut, and he had sparse patches of hair on his tanned skin. He actually looked perfect. "Well, Bobby is thin, and you can see his abdominal muscles. Steven, on the other hand, has some fat there, so you can't see the muscles."

"Very good description. Keep going."

"Okay, his belly hangs over his waist like a muffin."

"Exactly!" said Eric. "Okay, Michelle, you're next. I want you to critically examine the difference in their chests."

Also feeling bad but not daring to challenge Eric, Michelle began, "Well, again, Bobby's chest is toned and solid. Steven's looks a little droopy and even a bit like small breasts."

Eric turned to Steven. "Are boys supposed to have breasts? Don't answer—it's rhetorical."

This excruciating and awkward session examining each part of Steven's body went on for another ten minutes. By the end of the session, Steven just stood there and stared into the distance. They could tell he was doing everything in his power to fight back tears.

"You boys may step down now. Thank you all for your participation. Steven, I hope you can use this as motivation to get your life in order. You should spend less time eating and more time exercising. No one likes a fat boy. Okay, get changed and back to the bikes. We have twelve miles to go." Eric's mood suddenly seemed to change, and he put his arm around Steven and walked with him for a moment. "It will be okay, Steven. With hard work, you can look just like Bobby." Eric gave him a sympathetic pat on the back and then left to give him privacy to change.

That evening after reaching camp, they set up their tents. Each one could fit two people. The boys and girls paired up separately. Each counselor got their own tent. They built a fire and cooked hot dogs and baked beans for dinner. They sat around the fire afterward taking turns telling ghost stories. Eric must have been in a good mood because he was laughing and telling great stories. He passed out marshmallows, which they roasted on sticks over the open flame. Everyone had a good time, and Steven even laughed a bit at one of the jokes. You could tell Eric was going out of his way to be kind to Steven.

The next day after brushing their teeth and having dry cereal for breakfast, they boarded the bus for a quick ride to the Delaware River, where they would ride the canoes for twelve miles facing minimally challenging rapids. That day was fairly uneventful. There was only one occasion where the rapids became a little strong, and Sandy and Marvin's canoe got tossed sideways and then stuck between two large rocks. Everyone else had gone a little ahead of them and heard them screaming for help. Eric told everyone to tie up together and wait. He got out of his canoe and waded up the river in waist-deep water, eventually making it to where they were stuck. With his great strength he easily lifted the boat and corrected its position so that they could continue down to the rest of the group. While riding in their canoe, away from the ears of others, Jessica whispered to Bobby that he should come to her tent after everyone was asleep, and Dawn would go to Freddy's. The girls had talked about it and thought it would be so romantic to sleep in the same tent under the stars. Bobby was thrilled to hear it and knew that Freddy would be too.

That evening at the campsite, Bobby and Freddy positioned their tent adjacent to Jessica and Dawn's. That way, they could easily move from one to the other without discovery. While setting up the camp, they were startled when a shot rang out in the distance. Everyone looked at each other in alarm, but Adam calmed their fears. "Don't worry. Eric went out to catch us dinner."

About half an hour later, Eric walked back to the camp to huge applause carrying a small deer over his shoulders. "Tonight, we eat like kings!" His eyes looked wild, flashing from one camper to the next. There was blood splattered on his face and in his blond hair. He looked crazed. He went about preparing the meat and cooked it with the help of Adam and Serena.

When it was ready, they ate it with pasta on the side. It was delicious. It was so good to eat a fresh meal after spending two days in the wild.

That night when they sat around the fire, they told stories of their homes. They got on the subject of *Mary Poppins*, which had premiered last year.

"That was the first movie we saw on our brand-new color TV," said Steven.

"Whoa, you have a color TV in your home?" asked Charlie.

"Yeah, it was a Channukah present my dad gave us last December," he replied.

"Channukah?" asked Eric, not recognizing the word. "What's that?"

"It's the Jewish holiday that happens around the same time as Christmas every year," said Steven. "It lasts eight days, and we get a present each night. We also get to eat jelly donuts."

"Hmm," said Eric, glaring at Steven. "The fact that you eat jelly donuts, Steven, comes as little surprise to me. How many of the rest of you celebrate Chanukkah?"

Five other kids raised their hands, including Bobby, Freddy, and Jessica. "And who here celebrates Christmas?" The other six campers raised their hands. "Hmm, a pretty even mix here. I've noticed from camp office files that about half of our children are Christian, and half are Jews. I wonder why, when only two percent of our population are Jews, they make up fifty percent of the camp population? It makes you think."

No one else said anything, and the conversation returned to their favorite movies that came out that year. In truth, Bobby and Freddy could hardly think of anything else besides what might happen that night. As teenage boys, they had a one-track mind when it came to girls, and both were eager to take the next step. When they had been building their tents earlier, Bobby whispered to Freddy, "Did you bring the condoms?"

"Shit, no. Do you think they would let us if we had?"

"Jessica and I have become more adventurous lately, so I think she might."

"I don't know about Dawn. She gets so nervous when I try to put my hand under her clothes," said Freddy. "That would be epic if, as identical twins, we both got laid for the first time at the same time."

"Well, it's not going to happen without condoms anyway," said Bobby. "Do you even know how to use a condom?"

"Yeah, I've tried putting one on at home. I took one of Dad's," said Freddy.

"Oh, that's disgusting."

"It wasn't used."

"No, not that. It's disgusting to think of Dad and Mom doing it."

"Yeah," said Freddy. "Anyhow, you just rip open the wrapper and unroll it over your prick."

"Hey, do you think Adam has any on him?" asked Bobby. "He's pretty cool. I could ask him."

"Okay, do it quietly."

Bobby came back a few minutes later with one condom in a wrinkled wrapper. "He only had one."

"Shit. Well, I don't think Dawn is ready for that anyway."

When the storytelling was done around the fire, Eric told them all to go back to their tents, brush their teeth, and go to sleep.

Bobby and Freddy lay silently in their tent for what seemed like forever. They could hear the girls' tent being unzipped ever so slowly and quietly.

"Okay, she's coming," whispered Bobby.

"Good luck, brother. Don't fuck up, literally," he laughed and started to unzip their tent.

Jessica opened the boys' tent, and Freddy climbed out and into the girls' tent. Jessica took his vacant spot. She kissed Bobby. "I've been waiting for this for two days," she said. She pulled open his sleeping bag to climb in and was startled for a second to see him lying there naked. She paused for a second and climbed into his sleeping bag, where they embraced and kissed some more.

"I've been waiting for this my whole life," he replied.

He nervously fumbled with the condom, dropping it twice, which made Jessica giggle. Finally, after unwrapping it and rolling it on, he turned back to her, where they kissed some more. They tried to stay quiet out of fear of discovery, which Bobby almost ruined when he shot his leg out at one point, hitting the wall of the tent and making it shake. When they were finished, they lay sweating in each other's arms. She looked up at him. "I love you, Bobby."

"You too, Jess."

*

Jessica and Bobby had fallen asleep with their naked bodies intertwined. When morning arrived, she kissed Bobby awake. "We better get up before we're discovered together."

"I love you, Jessica."

"Love you too." She kissed him again before dressing and climbing out of the tent.

Freddy, who must have heard them stirring next door, was climbing out of Dawn's tent at the same time. Bobby came out of the tent next and walked with his brother into the woods to find a tree to pee on and then brush their teeth. Bobby and Freddy whispered about their nights. Freddy had a great time as well but did not get as far as Bobby. He listened carefully while Bobby told him all about what it was like to finally do it. Of course, he was envious of his brother but also felt so happy for him.

Dawn and Jessica must have been sharing details too because they were in a fit of laughter, and then both quieted down and blushed when they saw the boys coming back toward the campground. "Who wants breakfast?" asked Bobby, breaking the awkward silence.

The final day of the Grand Ohiwan was going to be made up of a series of three progressively harder rock faces to climb. Before the first climb, Eric discussed all of the safety equipment and protocols that were required to have a fun but safe day. Eric and the two counselors were all experienced rock climbers. Serena was responsible for putting on and checking the harness equipment for the girls, and Adam and Eric split the boys into two groups of four and helped them with their equipment.

The first climb was a thirty-foot rock face with multiple footholds and a more gradual angle. It was the kind of rock face that looked manageable even without safety equipment. Adam was the first to climb, and Eric was the belayer. The belayer controlled the safety rope for a climber and, in essence, was the final safety check that averted any potential catastrophe. Adam and Eric effectively demonstrated the proper technique. The girls set off to climb first. Then Adam took his set of four boys up the rock face. Eric's group was last to go. Bobby, Freddy, Steven, and Marvin made up Eric's group. They all easily achieved the first climb without any help from the belayer. Once reaching the top, the four boys traded high fives and smiles and began the short hike to the second rock face. They had to wait a while for Eric and the counselors to set up the safety ropes for the second face, which was about the same height and marginally steeper. The second climb was not much harder.

They reached the third rock face, which was a little taller

and steeper, with less obvious footholds. The boys looked up in awe at what was to come. Prior to the third climb, each of the groups sat down for lunch, which was peanut butter and jelly sandwiches again.

Sitting around at the bottom, the boys traded stories of their favorite baseball teams. All of the boys were from the NY area and were all Yankees fans. Steven, who was one of the younger kids on the Grand Ohiwan, was a huge fan of Mickey Mantle but he wanted to be a pitcher when he grew up. He'd pitched for his little league team this last spring. Marvin, who was on the team, was a good hitter and played center field. He was more agile and faster by far.

"Remember when I struck our Mikey Luka that last game? I was dealing!" said Steven.

"Yeah, you were," said Marvin. "I think that was the best game you've pitched. You're just lucky you didn't have to face me."

"I'd blow you away in three pitches," said Steven.

"Not a chance," laughed Marvin.

"Boys, you ready?" asked Eric.

"You bet we are!"

Eric redressed each boy in their harness and inspected it carefully. "Let's show the ladies how it's done. Boys, you're up. Do I have any volunteers to go first?"

They all looked at each other.

Eric scanned their faces. "How about you, Steven?"

"I'll do it!" said Steven bravely. Eric hooked him onto the line, and he began to climb. This was obviously a much more challenging rock face because Steven was taking a long time and was only about halfway up the forty-foot wall when he froze. The kids cheered him on and directed him where to find his next foothold and grip from below. He slowly made progress, making it about three-quarters of the way up the face. He tried to reach for the rock ledge, but as he grabbed it, the rocks came loose. With a piercing scream, he lost his grip and was now suspended in the air as Eric held him safely on the line.

"Calm down, Steven, I've got you," shouted Eric. "Now I want you to try and kick off the wall, and when you swing back, grab the ledge with your right hand. You can then continue to the top."

"No, please just lower me down. Please," Steven said with a wobbling voice, not listening to Eric's instructions.

"It's okay, Steven," said Adam. "Give me a moment. I'll climb up and show you how to do this."

"No, no, no, I just want to come down," cried Steven.

With a disgusted sneer, Eric gave in. "Okay, put your hand on the..."

Eric couldn't finish his sentence because suddenly, without warning, Steven came loose and fell for a split second before his foot got caught in the harness, suspending him upside down thirty feet from the ground. The campers screamed. Steven thrashed wildly in an attempt to reach the rope around his foot, screaming and sobbing hysterically.

"Stay calm!" demanded Eric.

Adam hooked on his safety rope and began to climb the face toward Steven. But it was too late. In an instant, his foot came loose, and Steven accelerated toward the earth. He crashed hard into the ground with a sickening thud and the sound of bones snapping. His head, hitting a rock, split open in two. He was fifteen years old, and he was dead.

Nine

Berlin 1938

"Well, from what I hear, your experience at camp was ter-rific," said David's mother. "From what David tells me, Eric, you were the star."

"Thank you, Aunt Barbara. David was also a star. He's very modest," replied Eric.

David, Emma, and Eric, along with their parents, all sat together for lunch in David's backyard. Barbara was serving lemonade to the teenagers and beer to the parents.

"Can we have a beer too, Uncle?" asked Eric.

"Yes, of course. Sorry, but I will always think of you as my cute little nephew running around the park with David. You too, Emma. You've all grown so fast," said Fredrick.

"David, what did you boys do at camp? Eric won't tell us much of anything," said Eric's mother, Jean.

"There's nothing to tell. It was camp. That's it. And it's a long time since we ran in the park as children. I have been assigned to work for the SS here in Berlin," said Eric.

"We're all so proud of you," said Eric's father, Barron. "But surely there was more to camp. What did you fill your days with? Emma, please tell us."

"We had very regimented days. We would wake up at six, brush our teeth, wash our face, and get dressed. Within twenty minutes we had to be out the door for morning roll call. Then it was exercise until eight thirty where we did calisthenics and marching. We then showered and went off to breakfast." Emma's voice was almost robotic. "The rest of the day we spent learning domestic skills such as cooking and cleaning. We also spent time in the classroom learning the science of the human race and ethnicity. Dancing and music were practiced in the afternoon. After dinner, I would finally have the chance to see Eric and David for some recreational time."

"You should see her room," said Emma's mother. "It's spotless. Her bed is perfectly made. It's like a whole new Emma."

"Yes, we noticed the same thing with Eric," said Jean. "He used to be a slob. Well, sorry, but you were. But now everything is total perfection. Never a wrinkle on his clothes or a stray hair on his head, nor dirty underwear lying in a heap on the ground."

"I'm sure you and Eric did not cook, clean, and practice your ballet all day," said Barron.

"No, of course not, Uncle," replied David. "We also had a regimented schedule, but our focus was more on sports, physical training, and even learning some military history and tactics. We learned to use weapons."

"Did you find any Jews to practice it on?" joked Emma's father. The three of them looked at each other, no one saying anything. The silence seemed to last an eternity.

Fredrick, alarmed, broke the silence. "You didn't, did you, David? Eric?"

"No, of course not, Uncle. As you say, we are still just children, after all."

Relieved, all of the parents began to laugh. "You gave us a scare for a moment," said Eric's mother.

"Anyway, what's the fuss if we did kill a Jew or two?" said Eric. "It's not like they're human. They crawl around our cities like rats, feeding on our good nature and using us for their own purposes. Hopefully, soon they will all leave Germany so we can prosper without them leeching off us."

"Hear, hear!" said Emma's father, raising his beer. "Well said, young man!"

Everyone raised a glass and drank their beer.

"Excuse me, I need the bathroom," said David as he hurried into the house.

*

Eric began his training with the SS one week later, while David and Emma returned to school. They did not see much of Eric while he was training. Occasionally they all got together, though Emma was feeling increasingly distant from him as he became more radicalized. She continued to keep him at arm's length when it came to sex.

Eric was one of eight new trainees selected to join a special force of SS officers under the command of its leader, Reichsführer Heinrich Himmler. Himmler was the thirty-eight-year-old commander of the entire Schutzstaffel, later called the SS. Adolf Hitler had appointed him to the position in 1929.

The SS started as a paramilitary organization in the early

1920s. When Himmler took command in 1929, the organization had less than three hundred members. He grew that number to over a million. It was broken down into several subgroups and was responsible for state security and surveillance. There were three main components of the SS: The General SS or the Allgemeine SS was for general policing and enforcement of racial laws. The Waffen SS was Hitler's combat branch. Finally, the SS Totenkopfverbände, under the command of Theodore Eicke, managed the death camps.

Eric was initially assigned to the General SS. He patrolled Berlin and participated in numerous raids on Hitler's political rivals. He followed tips and arrested conspirators and underground resistance personnel. He arrested and condemned numerous Germans, even on just rumors of treasonous thoughts. The speed and voracity of his arrests led to his continued distinction amongst the SS hierarchy. Finally, after just two months in Berlin, he was told that he was being sent to Dachau, a concentration camp, in order to assist Theodore Eicke.

One afternoon he caught up with David and Emma as they were leaving school. He was dressed in his full SS uniform, smoking a cigarette, and standing with his unit as they passed on the street with their heads down.

"Emma!" he called. She startled at first but relaxed when she realized it was Eric. David also turned around to see his cousin. He looked ferocious in his crisp uniform.

"I came here to say goodbye. I have been promoted and will be going to a work camp to help Commandant Eicke run it. He was appointed by the Führer himself, who will be coming to inspect the camps. Himmler thinks that I can help bring order and make things more efficient."

"Eric, we're so proud of you. You have become such an important person in the Reich," said David with a hint of false envy.

"I will miss you, David. I may not be able to return for some time. Please watch and protect Emma for me," said Eric. "Emma, I love you. Please wait for me." He bent over and kissed her. He tasted of tobacco.

"Please be careful, Eric. I'll miss you," she replied.

"I have nothing to fear," laughed Eric, patting his revolver. And with that, he climbed into the waiting truck and was off.

*

David and Emma spent every afternoon together after that. They never talked about their one night of passion. They both wanted to. They felt mixed emotions of longing for each other but also guilt over their betrayal of Eric.

One cool day in October, they were walking home together when Emma shuddered from the autumn chill. David took off his jacket and wrapped it around her shoulders.

"David, can we go somewhere to talk?" she asked. "How about here?" She nodded to the café opposite. "Let's go get coffee."

They ordered coffee and pastries and then sat at a table near the back.

"What's wrong, Emma?"

"David, do you ever think about that night by the fire?"

"I feel so terrible about that," said David. "I've been wanting to apologize to you. I've been wanting to apologize to Eric."

"No! You can never tell him. He would never forgive us."

"I know, but it's eating at me. It makes me sick to think I would do that to my cousin and lifelong friend," he said.

"Did you like it?" she asked sheepishly.

"Emma, of course I did." He took her hand. "That was the first time I ever, you know, did that. You have always been such a dear friend, but to be honest, I've been envious of your relationship with Eric. I think I fell for you the same time Eric did, but he got you first."

Emma's cheeks turned pink. "I liked it too. I really like you, David," she said. "But it's very complicated. You know I have become frightened of him, and I don't feel comfortable with him. I don't think I love him anymore."

"But, Emma, we could never work. What would Eric do if he found out?"

"It's worse than that, David," said Emma.

"What's worse?"

"You see, I never let Eric sleep with me the way we did. I was a virgin until that night. Even after that night, I never slept with Eric."

David blushed. He couldn't believe what he was hearing. Did she actually prefer him to Eric? And she had been a virgin too? He had always imagined that she and Eric were having sex.

"David, there's more," continued Emma, bringing him back from his thoughts. "I don't know how to say it, so I just will."

"What is it, Emma?"

"I'm pregnant."

Ten

Camp Ohiwa 1965

After returning from the Grand Ohiwan, everything was different. In years past, the campers would return to their bunks, shower, nap, and then be treated to a grand celebration that night. The members would triumphantly walk across the stage in the mess hall, where stories of their bravery would be announced. Then there would be a feast including all-you-can-eat ice cream for the campers. This year was completely different.

This year the group returned with one less camper than when they'd left. They spent the whole third day at the mountainside. After the fall, Adam and Serena ran to Steven and tried to rouse him. It really was a bloody mess. He lay there in a position that even anyone without medical training could tell was incompatible with life. His torso lay perpendicular to the rock face, and his right arm was bent back and behind his body, almost as if he'd tried to break the fall. His shoulder must have shattered like a piece of glass. His left arm was out to the side. His neck was clearly broken, judging from how his head was positioned away from his chest. But worst of all was his head. In between the overgrown red curls, you could see his head had been split in two by the rock he'd landed on. Blood was still coming out, and gray material, possibly his brain, was exposed too. Steven's green eyes and mouth were wide open. The frightened panic at the last moments would be his death mask. Besides the counselors, who were assessing him, everyone else was either crying or in silent shock. Jessica couldn't stop convulsing in tears. Bobby tried to comfort her.

"Leave him! He's dead," said Eric. "It will do no good to fuss any further. Adam, hike up to where the bus is waiting and call for an ambulance."

The campers ended up sitting around for almost two hours. They tried to comfort each other. They tried to make sense of what had just happened. A fifteen-year-old boy just fell thirty feet and cracked his skull open while having fun at summer camp. And died! Why?

"His harness must have been secured wrong," said Serena.

"No! His harness was completely correct. I double-checked it myself. He panicked, jerked his body backward for some unknown reason, and slipped right out. If only he'd listened to simple instructions, he wouldn't be lying dead on the forest floor," responded Eric.

The ambulance and the police arrived. They talked only to Eric and took pictures of the body before putting it in a body bag and carrying it away. That was the last they heard of Steven.

When they got back to camp, they expected to have a ceremony or be given some sort of closure on what happened, but it was never addressed, save for one moment. That night at dinner, Eric greeted the campers and congratulated them briefly on completing the Grand Ohiwan. Then he said, "Unfortunately, one of our other campers, Steven, won't be returning. There was a tragic accident due to him being overweight and not following instructions."

That was all he ever said about it. Of course, word spread amongst the campers, and by the next day, everyone knew what had happened. It created a deep sadness in the camp, almost as if someone had pulled a great gray fog over it and left it there.

The daily activities continued, but all of the fun was over. Bobby didn't even have a chance to process what had happened with Jessica in the tent that night. He'd lost his virginity to the girl he loved, and it had been a perfect night. They were both inexperienced, and it was awkward, but it was also perfect. They had kissed and explored each other's bodies. Afterward, they talked for a while and eventually fell asleep in each other's arms. They had seen each other just a couple of times since they returned. They smiled at each other and made small talk, but neither dared to talk about that night at all. No one was thinking of anything other than poor Steven.

Things seemed to remain in a lull for the next two weeks. The activities and meals continued on, but no one was really having any fun. In fact, campers were bickering more and more about what was lacking instead of enjoying what remained of the summer.

One Friday evening, with only three weeks left of camp, Eric asked all of the campers to join him in the amphitheater instead of heading to dinner. It was the beginning of a night full of surprises. When they arrived at the outdoor theater, they could see immediately that this was going to be a special night. There were tables along the edges of the theater with buckets filled with every sort of candy you could imagine. On each table were six tubs filled with different flavors of ice cream. There was whipped cream, cherries, sprinkles, hot fudge, and caramel sauce. On Bobby's first pass down the aisle, he took a scoop of chocolate, mint chocolate chip, and rocky road and covered it with whipped cream, sprinkles, and a cherry. He sat with Dawn, Freddy, and Jessica. The theater was buzzing with anticipation of what was to come. As the sun set, the counselors started passing out McDonald's burgers and nuggets. They pigged out.

Suddenly, *bang, bang, bang,* and the sky lit up with fireworks. Music came on in the background, but no one could place it. It sounded like a national anthem but not "The Star-Spangled Banner." It was in a foreign language that was not obviously Spanish or French. The fireworks stopped, and the music came to an end.

Floodlights came on, directed at a podium where Eric was standing at attention wearing a green-gray uniform with black shoes and multiple medals on his lapel. His hat was green, and there was a silver bird at the front.

"Silence. Silence!" Eric repeated. "Please sit down."

They all obeyed. Bobby looked back and forth between Jessica and Freddy, who returned his gaze with an equally quizzical expression.

"I hope you have enjoyed your ice cream dinner and special surprises that followed. I know the mood in camp has been down since the unfortunate accident on the Grand Ohiwan. Yes, it was tragic. But we need to move on. If we dwell on all the bad in life, we will never be able to enjoy the good. With that in mind, I wanted to announce that we will be having an extra special color wars this year. The first part of the week will be traditional. I will separate the entire camp into two teams. Each team will compete in a series of Olympic-style games. I will test your strength, stamina, skill, and resourcefulness over two days. At the end of the two days the dominant group will be crowned and the weak group will watch. But that is not the end. That is just where the fun will begin. On day three we will take the two groups and play a sort of 'cops and robbers,' if you will. The winning team will be the cops or guards and the losing team will be the prisoners. Then we will have many surprises and competitions with high stakes. How does that sound?"

The campers looked around with excitement. This was the change they needed. They had been sad and bored ever since their return but the idea of a new color wars was exciting. What would the cops and robbers portion look like? Everyone began to cheer.

Eric raised his arm, silencing the crowd again. "I knew you would like my new games. They will be to die for." He laughed. "You may be wondering who will be on the red team and who will be on the yellow team. I have changed that too. To make it a little more fun I will separate the two teams as such. For our Jew campers, you will be on the yellow team. Our non-Jew campers will be on the red team."

Eleven

Berlin 1942

The prisoners were lined up in the courtyard against the brick façade at the SS post in Berlin. Wilhelm Kruger, captain of the local SS police headquarters, marched up and down the row. Eric Bauer stood at attention in front of the prisoners. He had been home for the last few days and events had unfolded very quickly. This was his first time home in nearly four years. He had done very well at Dachau. So much so that he was moved from camp to camp, helping to organize them. What were initially just labor camps had turned into death factories. The goal was the elimination of the European Jewry and all of the other undesirables including gypsies, homosexuals, disabled Germans, and Hitler's political opponents.

As Wilhelm Kruger came to a stop across from the captives, he calmly said, "The Jews among you today will be relocated to Auschwitz. It is a lovely camp in Poland. I'm sure you will find it very much to your liking. For the criminals who conspired to hide the Jews, you shall be executed." With this, Eric's mother made an audible sigh and passed out.

A few days earlier, Eric had returned to Berlin for several

meetings with Himmler, Heydrich, and Hitler. His notoriety within the Reich had grown. His leadership was renowned for its efficiency and brutality. Himmler, very pleased with his work, continued to elevate him within the Reich. He was now an integral part in the formation of what later became known as the Final Solution.

Eric had not been in touch with David or his family for years. Nor had he spoken to Emma, aside from the occasional letters that he would send her. They were always short. He kept her up to date with all of his promotions and kept the sordid details of what he was doing to himself. The letters would always end with, "I long for the day we will be together again and can start our life together. Fondly, Eric." Since he was always on the move, it was not possible for Emma to respond. Despite not seeing her, Emma was never far from his thoughts. He imagined a joyful reunion. He had remained true to Emma. That is not to say that he did not take a woman from time to time. He frequently slept with German girls and occasionally raped his prisoners, but that was more a form of torture for them than any enjoyment for him, or so he thought. But he never considered any of them his girlfriend. His plan, once he was done doing his duty for the fatherland, was to return to Berlin and marry his sweetheart. Such was the life of an SS officer during the war. There simply wasn't any time to return to Berlin except on business, and this was his first chance. He rode the train for four hours.

Eric loved the respect he commanded on the train. He always traveled in his full SS gear. As he walked down the aisle, several people offered him their seats, but he just ignored them and walked on. He came across an older man traveling with his daughter. She must have been about eighteen. She was thin with long straight red hair that curled at the ends. She kept her gaze down. Her father, a man in his fifties with prematurely white hair, looked up and smiled at Eric. He saluted Eric with the traditional "Heil Hitler."

"Heil Hitler," Eric responded. "I would like your seat."

"Yes, of course, sir," said the older man, getting up. "We will find another place. Come on, Bertha."

"No," Eric said in a calm but firm manner. "She will remain here with me. Just you leave. Now."

"Sir, my daughter is traveling with me. We do not want any trouble," pleaded the father.

"There will be no trouble. Now go find another seat. I will watch your daughter very carefully," said Eric, staring at the man with one hand moving to his pistol.

The older man got up and moved to another area, and Eric took his place next to the young girl. He sat very close to her, pushing the side of his body against her. She moved away as best she could, squishing herself against the window.

"Bertha is a very pretty name. It goes well with such a pretty girl."

"Thank you, sir," she whispered.

"Don't be afraid of me. You may call me Eric. Where are you and your father traveling to?"

"We are going to see my grandmother. She lives in Berlin and has been very sick," said Bertha.

"I'm sorry to hear that, Bertha," replied Eric in his sweetest voice as he put his left hand on the inside of her thigh.

"Please, sir," she said.

"It's Eric."

"Please, Eric. I am engaged to be married."

"And who is the lucky boy?" asked Eric as he continued to move his hand up her leg.

"His name is Johann," she said as tears started rolling down her cheeks.

"Where is Johann?"

"He's stationed in Poland. He fights in the army."

"Well, let's hope he doesn't get killed," said Eric, watching her as tears continued to roll down her face. "You know you are far too pretty to cry like that. It will ruin your makeup." Keeping one hand on her leg, he leaned in and with one long motion licked the tear from the side of her mouth up to just below her eye.

Beyond frightened, she sat motionless, staring straight ahead.

"Well, good day, Bertha," said Eric as he abruptly stood up and continued to walk down the train looking for another place to sit.

He came to another group of seats occupied by some Hitler Youth children. They all stood up and saluted him. "Heil Hitler," they shouted. He returned the salute and then sent them away, taking the entire four seats for himself. He looked out the window and daydreamed about his youth. It had been much simpler. He smiled as he remembered skinny dipping with Emma and David. It was all so fun and new then. Each experience was a first. He wondered what his cousin was up to and how his parents were managing. As family members of a high-ranking SS officer, he knew that they were well treated and had access to everything they needed. They would also be able to acquire some of the more luxurious items that general German citizens found increasingly scarce as the war went on.

Arriving at the station in Berlin, he decided to go straight to Emma's house. It had been almost four years and he couldn't wait even another few hours. He would take her to dinner and then they would stay at a five-star hotel, drink champagne, and make love. Then he would ask her to marry him. She was going to be so impressed with his status and rank within the Reich. He would set her up in a penthouse apartment that was commandeered from a Jewish family after being sent to a death camp. There were numerous vacancies throughout Berlin and he could have his pick for free.

He arrived at Emma's house and knocked loudly on the door. He repeated knocking and after a few minutes Emma's housekeeper appeared at the door.

"Sir, can I help you?" she asked.

"Emma, please," requested Eric.

"She doesn't live here anymore," said the housekeeper.

"Where does she live?"

"I don't know her new address."

"And her parents?"

"Her father lives here but he is not home."

"Where is her mother?"

"Oh, sir. She died over a year ago."

"How? She wasn't sick. What happened?"

"She was killed by a car that lost control and hit her in the market."

Eric paused for a moment, thinking of Emma's mother. Poor Emma. She must have been devastated.

"Where is her father?"

"I don't know, sir, he didn't say."

Eric, growing angry now, unholstered his gun and said, "Tell me right now. Do you know who I am? I will have you arrested if you don't take me to him at once."

Trembling, she said, "He is probably at the bar at the corner by the deli. That is where he goes most nights."

Eric stormed off to find Emma's father. It didn't take him long to reach the corner bar. He wrenched open the door, and the room grew quiet seeing a high-ranking Nazi officer come in. He scanned the room. There were three men sitting at the bar, which was being tended by a pretty girl. Her blue dress was cut low in front, exposing the skin around the top of her chest. A couple of people were sitting at various tables. Three junior SS officers immediately stood to attention upon seeing Eric. "Heil Hitler," they said, saluting him.

"Heil Hitler," responded Eric dismissively. Finally, he spotted Emma's father sitting alone at a small table in the corner. He walked over to Peter, who didn't seem to notice him coming. He was staring down at his beer. Eric pulled out a chair and sat down across from him.

"Eric, is that you?" asked Peter, slurring his words. He was clearly quite drunk and looked fat, red-faced, and pathetic to Eric.

"What happened to you?" asked Eric.

"Life happened. My darling wife was..." His words trailed off. He picked up his beer and took another long swig. "She was coming home from the market when a drunk man in the middle of the day lost control of his car and hit her. She was killed instantly, or so I'm told. She never even saw it coming.

Must be for the best. She was so depressed with, well, you know."

"No, I don't know," said Eric. "Why was she depressed? Germany is doing so well. Hitler has us on track to have all of Europe within a few years."

"No, she was so upset because of Emma," said Peter.

"Emma? What happened to Emma? Is she okay?"

"Oh, she is okay. Quite healthy in fact. We haven't spoken to her for years, not since a few months after you left. She had come over one evening with your cousin David. They were holding hands as we sat in the living room."

Eric's heart began to pound hearing this. Had she been untrue to him? And with David? His cousin would never do that to him. Would he?

"Go on!" said Eric. "And try not to slur your words, you disgusting drunk!"

"Well, she told us that they wanted to discuss something very important and implored us to listen to everything before saying a word. Emma was four months pregnant."

Eric felt the blood drain from his face. He turned and shouted at the waitress to bring him two beers. "Go on!"

"They wanted our permission to marry so that the child she was carrying would be legitimate. We always thought that Emma would end up with you. We had known all three of you since you were children. But David was a nice boy as well. Of course, we were disappointed that they had, uh, slept together before, well, before being married. We didn't live with our heads in the sand either though. We were young once too. Her mother was happy for them. She liked David very much. Like I said, we were very surprised though that it wasn't you.

You had a much more promising career. Look at you now. A high-ranking Nazi."

"The highest ranking, you drunken slob! I work with Himmler and even the Führer himself. And your daughter, that whore! With David?" screamed Eric, spit coming out with each word.

When Eric's tirade petered out the two men sat there in silence drinking their beer.

After a few minutes, Emma's father continued, "Of course, David has a good career as well. Because his father runs the bank, David was needed and therefore was not made to join the army. I'm told he does quite well now. They bought a two-story home downtown near the park. They live there with the child, a nanny, and a housekeeper."

"So why haven't you spoken to her in years?" asked Eric.

"After discussing the pregnancy and their plans for marriage we of course came around and granted them permission. After the wedding, which was just a few weeks later, Emma and David came to us again to discuss something important. We said what could be so important that it requires a second discussion? David said that he had a secret to discuss with us since we were all family now and he wanted to be honest with us from the start. So, he told us the secret. We were so disgusted. We were beside ourselves. Not only would his secret put Emma at risk, but it would also put us and their baby at risk. How could she be so stupid? We told her she should get divorced right away and when she refused, we told her she was no longer our daughter. They tried several times again to contact us but we always refused."

"What secret?" demanded Eric.

"You know it, Eric. You're his cousin," said Peter.

"What are you talking about?"

"Stop playing, Eric. The secret that David is half Jew. Of course, we never reported them out of fear that they would all be arrested and sent to a death camp, but as far as we were concerned, she was dead to us anyway."

"Jew? David's a Jew? Impossible!" Eric stood up. "Where do they live now? I must see them at once."

Twelve

Berlin 1942

David, Emma, and their three-year-old boy Otto had just arrived at David's parents' house along with Peter, Emma's father.

"What's wrong?" said Barbara as she opened the door to let them in.

"Granny!" shouted Otto, as he ran and jumped into his grandmother's arms.

She smiled and kissed him. Her smile faded when Peter walked through the door. They all had been estranged from Peter for years now. Peter and David set down three small suitcases.

"Where's Dad? Get him quickly!" said David.

"What happened? Please tell me. You're worrying me."

"Come, let's sit down. Get Father, please."

Fredrick walked into the room and saw Peter, David, Emma, and Barbara all sitting there, nervously watching Otto play with his teddy bear on the floor.

"What has happened?" asked Fredrick.

"It is all my fault," said Peter. "Last night I was sitting in the bar and had, well, one too many beers. I was minding my own business when in walked Eric. He had just returned from a meeting at the work camp. I hadn't seen or heard from him in years. He started asking about Emma. Apparently, he hasn't been in communication with our children either for the last few years and was shocked when I told him that David and Emma were married and had a child."

"How is Eric? Is he healthy? Is he doing well?" asked Barbara. "I have always thought of my nephew as like another of my sons."

"Yes, yes! He's fine and healthy. But he is a very high-ranking Nazi now. He told me he was going to meet with the Führer personally this week."

"Oh my," said Fredrick. "Is he coming to visit us too?"

"Well, that's the problem," responded Peter. "It seems that I have a big mouth and mentioned that David is half Jew. I didn't know he was left out of that secret."

There was silence in the room.

"How did he react?" asked Barbara. "I'm sure we don't have anything to worry about. He wouldn't turn us in. Not Eric. We're his family."

"I don't know about that," said Peter. "Eric has changed. I have never seen such a crazed look of hatred in a man. When I woke up early this morning and realized what I had done, I went straight to warn David and Emma. What have I done? What have I done?" Peter began to sob. "I'm so sorry. I've ruined everything."

"Mother, Father. I think we all need to leave right away," said David, looking ashen. "I packed lightly for the three of us and brought all the cash I had in our home. We have documents too. We must leave for Switzerland immediately. Tonight."

"Yes, I agree," Fredrick uttered quietly. "We must go right away. Barbara, pack just essentials. I'll get the papers and our money. Bring your wedding ring and your necklace too. I have enough cash on hand to set us up once we reach Switzerland."

"What about Samuel?" asked Barbara. "We have no way of warning him. Last I heard he was fighting the Russians to the east. Peter, please ask my sister Jean to send Samuel a letter letting him know that the secret's out and we've left to visit Aunt Elda. He will know what that means."

Barbara and Fredrick quickly got up to begin getting their bags together.

"Emma, David, I'm so sorry. Not just for this but for how we treated you. I was blinded by my hatred. Your mother didn't agree. It tormented her to treat you like we did but she was obedient to me," said Peter.

"Oh, Papa," replied Emma, standing up and walking to him. She embraced her father. Tears were rolling down his face. The years had not served him well. He had grown old, his shoulders slumped and rounded from spending too much time hunched over a beer.

"May I meet my grandson? He looks just like you when you were a small girl."

At that moment, there was a loud knock at the door.

"Are you expecting anyone?" asked Emma.

"No," said Barbara. "Just stay quiet. Maybe they will go away."

The banging got louder. "SS! Open now or we will break the door."

They looked at each other in fear. No one could move. When the banging got louder, Barbara walked to the door. "Stay here. I will tell them no one is home."

Barbara opened the door a fraction. "Can I help—"

Seven SS troopers pushed past her and quickly made their way through the house, tracking mud along the clean wood floors and fine silk carpets.

"What are you doing in my house?" cried Fredrick. "You must leave at once."

They ignored him and pushed him back into the wall. One of the SS troopers hit him in the face with the back of his rifle. Blood gushed down his face. Barbara shrieked.

"You will pay for that," said Fredrick. "Do you know who I am? I run the largest bank in Germany and I report directly to the Minister of Finance. You will be whipped for your impudence."

"Shut up, old man, and sit down or next time it's really going to hurt," replied the officer.

They rounded up the family and forced them to sit quietly on the couch. Otto began to cry. "Silence the little rat or I will," said the SS officer, taking his gun from his pocket.

"Please, no," cried David, standing up to comfort Otto. One of the officers hit David across his shin with a baton. He fell to the floor with a loud thud.

Emma picked up Otto and whispered a gentle lullaby in his ear while combing her fingers through his hair. This calmed and quieted him. David picked himself up and sat down next to Emma.

They waited in silence for what seemed to be an eternity. It was perfectly quiet except for some muffled sobs coming from

Barbara as Fredrick tried to comfort her. Then they heard approaching footsteps coming toward them. In walked Eric, tall, blond, with a perfectly pressed SS captain's uniform.

"Heil Hitler," the men saluted him. "All of the prisoners are here, sir."

"Heil Hitler," he said in a slow calculating tone, his blue eyes cold.

"Eric, thank God it's you," said Emma. "These men have rounded us up like prisoners." She got up to hug him but was pushed back into place by one of the men. Eric looked at each of them. Emma had become more beautiful than ever. Even wearing her traveling clothes, he could see how she had developed into an even more irresistible woman. David looked very similar and it made his head hurt seeing him holding her. And that little boy with his chubby face and blond curls. He looked like he could have been his own son. He should have been his son but of course it couldn't be. He looked at his aunt and uncle cowering in the corner. His uncle, the filthy Jew who had been hiding his identity while becoming rich off the backs of Germans. He wondered what he did with all that money. Probably supported the council of elders, the Jewish group that had secretly run the world, he thought.

"Eric, please help us," cried Emma.

He turned to his SS troopers and said, "This is all of them. Take them in." And with that he turned on his heel and marched out.

"Eric, please!" she cried, but to no avail. Her pleas fell on deaf ears.

*

David, Emma, Otto, David's parents, and Emma's father

were held at the cell at the SS station in Berlin for three days. They were all kept in a single cell, with a single cot. Emma and Barbara took turns resting on the cot while the men slept on the floor. Otto stayed with his mother. They were fed just once a day. The portions were small and made up of stale bread and cabbage soup. There was no bathroom, just a bucket in the corner of the room that was emptied once a day. For them this was a total humiliation. As a wealthy bank executive, Fredrick and his family had always enjoyed luxuries, and now being forced to expel their waste without even a curtain for modesty was mortifying. The smell of unwashed bodies, bad breath, and human waste was almost unbearable. Late one evening the cell door opened with a bang, startling the family.

"Up! Up!" shouted the guard. They were led out to a court-yard in the center of the building. There was a floodlight illuminating the brick wall. In front of the wall already standing at attention were Eric's mother and father, Jean and Barron. The family was made to line up in front of the wall.

As Wilhelm Kruger came to a stop across from the captives he calmly said, "The Jews among you today will be relocated to Auschwitz. It is a lovely camp in Poland. I'm sure you will find it very much to your liking. For the criminals who conspired to hide the Jews, you shall be executed."

Upon hearing this, Eric's mother suddenly collapsed. Barron helped her back to her feet.

"Eric," cried his mother, "what is happening? Why are they doing this to us?"

"Mother, Father, I am very sorry you chose to act against the Reich. Knowing full well that David and his father are

Jews, you decided not to report them to the Reich and instead harbor them. There is no worse sin for a German than to go against our country and our Führer," said Eric. "As my parents, you have been given all of the privileges due to my rank and you betrayed me. How does it make me look to my Führer that my own uncle and cousin are Jews and that my parents protected them? There can be no mercy for you."

With his mother pleading and crying, his father just stood there, staring him in the eyes. He had the look of complete failure that his son could turn on his own family like this. Meeting his father's stare, Eric suddenly felt strangely sad and guilty. How could he order the death of his own parents? But what would Hitler think of him if he chose his family over the Reich? His eyes began to water. "It's your own damn fault. Don't blame me! Goodbye, Mother and Father."

With that, Eric turned to Wilhelm Kruger and nodded.

"As enemies of the Reich, Barron and Jean Bauer, you are sentenced to death. Furthermore, Peter Von Hinder, as you failed to report these Jews, you are also sentenced to death," said Kruger.

Emma gasped. David held her tightly.

The three of them were tied to wood posts against the brick wall.

"On my command," shouted Kruger, as the guards raised their rifles. "Fire!"

Eric did not even flinch as his mother and father fell to their knees, supported only by their hands tied to the post. All three were dead in an instant.

Eric turned his attention now to Emma and David's child.

"Why have my wife and son been detained?" shouted Eric.

"I gave strict orders for them to be given comfortable housing while waiting for my return."

Emma turned to David in alarm but he just gave her a reassuring look.

"I'm sorry, sir. I thought the child belonged to the Jew," said one of the guards.

"Of course he doesn't belong to the Jew. He is my son! Does he look like a filthy Jew? David, thank you for watching my child and supporting my wife while I've been gone. I was very troubled to learn that you are a Jew. We grew up together and never once did you tell me. I feel so dishonored by what you have done. You were my best friend," said Eric.

"Eric, please let me explain," protested David.

"Silence, Jew," shouted Eric.

Eric again looked at Kruger. "You may take them away now."

The guards led David and his parents out the door and onto a truck bound for the train station.

"Don't worry, David," said Eric, as he grabbed Emma, putting his arms around her waist. "My wife and son will be coming with me to my new posting at Auschwitz. Perhaps we will see you there."

Thirteen

Camp Ohiwa 1965

On the Monday of the second to last week of camp, color wars was set to begin. Everyone was excited about the new format and what the "cops and robbers" part of it might be. It was a little strange, however, about the Jew versus non-Jew part. Why would Eric separate the groups by religion? The world was still recovering from the Second World War and Bobby's parents had told him countless stories about the difficulties and horrors that Jews faced just twenty years ago. But as strange as it was, the Jewish campers also embraced it. They would be like the Maccabees, who were a group of Jewish soldiers two thousand years ago who overcame the powerful Seleucid empire. They had learned about it in Hebrew school on Sunday mornings. Besides Bobby, Freddy, and Jessica, Jonathan, Marvin, and Sandy were on the Jewish team. Notable friends on the non-Jewish team were Dawn and Harris. Each team was given a captain. For the yellow team, counselor Adam was designated captain and for the red team a counselor named Joseph would be the captain.

There were about sixty children on each team ranging in

age from eight to fifteen. The yellow team was lined up on the left and the red team was on the right. Everyone had a big smile on their face, anxious for the games to begin. Eric stepped up to the podium next to his son, Otto. The man, probably in his mid-twenties, was tall and muscular but not as tall as Eric. He had dirty blond hair and a kind smile.

"Good morning, Camp Ohiwa, and welcome to the new edition of color wars!" announced Eric.

Everyone cheered.

"As I mentioned before, this year we will have a new format. Today marks the beginning of the first part of the color wars week. Here to describe today's events is my son, Otto."

Otto stepped forward and began to describe what was to come. He had a strong voice but without the harsh accent of his father. Today there was going to be a series of sporting events. First would be capture the flag. Then would come relay races, hurdles, archery, and rifle range competitions. After lunch would be soccer. The games would be broken down by age and team captains would assign the campers in such a way so as to give their teams the best chance of winning. The second day would be for water sports. There would be several straight swimming competitions as well as relay races. There would also be diving competitions and water polo.

Otto continued, "To get into the spirit of the competition, teams will eat and sleep together and should not communicate with the enemy team. Anyone caught breaking these rules of spirit will be docked a point toward the final tallies. Before starting, the teams will break up into smaller groups and you will vote on one of the fight songs my father created for each team. You will adopt that song and sing it before every match. Are there any questions? Okay, if not then meet back at the fields at ten a.m. for our first game—capture the flag. Dismissed!"

The choices weren't great for the yellow team but they ultimately decided on this song.

From dawn till dusk, we'll give it our all
We may not be strong but we'll stand tall
We work together to control our fate
Yellow, Yellow, do not hesitate.

The red team picked their favorite of the choices Eric created as well.

Beware of the crooked
Beware of the Jew
Cover your belongings
Or they will steal from you!
Go Red, Go Red
If they won't stop, make them dead!

The campers on the yellow team wore all yellow and the red team wore all red but they somehow got their hands on some red paint too. They put it on their faces and sprayed their hair with it as well. Some of the boys played their sports topless and painted their chests red. They looked tough and the red paint seemed to give them a psychological edge. It seemed to put them more in character for being at war.

Over the next two days yellow competed hard against the red team. An official tally was never offered but at one point at the end of day one they were told the scores were very close, with one team having sixty-three points and the other sixty-five. It was still anyone's game. Freddy and Bobby competed in the relay race and the freestyle swim race and won both. The red team seemed to be better organized when it came to the group games and they easily beat yellow in capture the flag, soccer, and water polo. Bobby felt strange seeing his friends on the other team and not being able to talk to them. He saw Freddy and Dawn exchange smiles but didn't dare talk. No one wanted to risk losing points and being the cause of their team's failure.

In the evening while sitting for announcements, Eric said that there were two very serious infractions. "It has come to my attention that several members of the yellow team were caught stealing cookies and soda from the pantry and distributing it amongst their teammates. Additionally, two of the counselors on the red team witnessed two of the boys from the yellow team relieving themselves on the door to one of the red bunks. Now it is understandable that the yellow team has become frustrated with their lack of innate abilities compared to the members of the red team but that does not excuse this behavior."

The campers on the yellow team looked to each other with bewilderment. Shouts of "We didn't do it!" could be heard from several of the children.

"Silence!" shouted Eric as he banged his fist on the podium. "Because of these acts there will be punishments handed out. There will be no dinner tonight. You will all return to your bunks and go to sleep. The morning activities will be can- celed and instead we will be waking up at four a.m. to begin running, sit-ups, pushups, and burpees. Additionally, there will be no more desserts for the remainder of the week."

Some of the red team members could be heard snickering at the yellow team. Others were slapping high fives.

"Don't look so pleased with yourselves!" Eric turned his ire on the red team. "These punishments will also go to the red team."

"What? We didn't do anything!" shouted one of the red team campers.

"Exactly!" said Eric. "You are all members of our camp society and you chose to let the yellow team commit these treacherous acts. Not one of you stepped up to stop them. So, you are all guilty. Perhaps in the future you will remember that you all have a responsibility to ensure order."

Campers on both sides were frustrated and angry. On the yellow team's part, they were pretty sure that these infractions were all fabricated. The red campers were angry that some stupid yellow campers' actions had ruined their good time. They were also incredulous that the yellow team would pee on their cabins.

When the yellow team passed members on the red team the following morning it seemed like they were taking it very seriously. Bobby noted hatred in their eyes. The yellow team also began to feel anger toward their fellow campers especially when they would celebrate at their expense. They were playing their parts in this color war. As each competition went on the teams felt more and more like they were actually at war.

At the end of the day, they gathered in the large mess hall, yellow on one side, red on the other.

Eric began, "Congratulations on a very hard-fought and spirited competition. I have to admit that I am surprised how well the yellow team handled themselves. But in the end, it is not about trying hard but about results. There are winners and losers and nothing in between. The winner of this year's color wars is the red team. The Jews are the losers."

Yellow team sat back, dejected in their defeat, and watched as the red team jumped to their feet screaming. It started as a chaotic mumble but grew into a loud chorus.

"Beware of the crooked
Beware of the Jew
Cover your belongings
Or they will steal from you!
Go Red, Go Red
If they won't stop, make them dead!

"Beware of the crooked
Beware of the Jew
Cover your belongings
Or they will steal from you!
Go Red, Go Red
If they won't stop, make them dead!"

They repeated themselves over and over and over until Eric took the podium again.

"Now the real fun can begin. For the next five days, the red team will be the guards and the yellow team will be the prisoners. There will be more competitions and lots of fun to be had. The red team can go back to the bunks and shower.

Yellow team will stay and sleep here in the mess hall as a group. Tomorrow morning, we begin at dawn on the fields for roll call. Do not be late."

The yellow team campers looked at each other in surprise. What did Eric mean? Would they be held in captivity and sleep here in the mess hall? Sleep on what? Bobby found Freddy, Jessica, and Jonathan sitting a couple of tables down.

"They've got to be joking, right?" Bobby asked.

"Yes. I'm going back to our bunk," said Freddy.

"We should probably call Dad. This has gone too far. 'Beware of the Jew?' This isn't 1930s Germany. It's 1960s America," Bobby said.

"I'm scared," said Jessica, grabbing his hand.

"Come on, let's go call my dad and then go back to the bunk."

"Bobby, the phone is still out. I tried it last week but no one's come to repair it yet," said Jonathan.

Looking around, they could see all of the scared faces of the younger children. Adam and Seth, the two counselors from the Jewish team, were also there wearing their yellow shirts. They were moving the tables to one side of the mess hall to make room for the children to lie on the floor and try to sleep for the night.

"Let's go talk to Adam," Bobby suggested.

When they found Adam, they asked what was going on and if this was a big joke.

He looked back at them with a worried look.

"I think they're serious," he said. "I spoke to Otto before and he said that his father was dead serious about changing the culture here. He said that Eric had been depressed for many years after the war but he seems to have been 'reborn' here at Camp Ohiwa. His father feels Americans have lost their discipline and that society is again crumbling. He even heard him blame the Jews. He said that his father compared 1960s America to the fall of Germany and he feels Jews are responsible again."

"What did you say to Otto?" asked Bobby.

"I said that I didn't think it was right to separate the color wars teams by religion. I thought it would lead to bad feelings. Otto said he thought his father was wrong too but he would never oppose him. Apparently, he had tried to question him but Eric hit him so hard with a backhand across the face he felt like his jaw had broken."

Jessica let out a gasp and Bobby squeezed her hand tighter.

"Anyhow, I guess you guys should try to find some space on the floor. It's getting late. We have to be up for roll call in the morning and see what kind of games the day will bring."

"I'm not sleeping here on the floor," said Jessica. "I don't have my toothbrush or a change of clothes."

"We're all in the same boat. These are the rules of the game," responded Adam.

"Adam, we need to call someone for help. Is there another phone?" Bobby asked.

"The only working phone is in the director's office. But he's not going to let you in."

"I noticed the window to his office is usually open. Maybe one of us could get in there and make the call," said Freddy.

"But first we have to get out of here," Bobby replied.

"Let's go. I'm walking straight out that door and I'm going

to sleep in my bunk on my bed. Tonight, one of you boys should sneak out and make the call," said Jessica.

"We're coming with you," said Bobby.

After ignoring Adam's protests, they walked up to the front door of the mess hall but it was locked.

"What the fuck!" Freddy screamed. They tried the back entrance but it was also locked. Going back to the front, they began pounding on the door. After a few moments the door opened and one of the counselors in a red shirt asked what they wanted. There were four other big boys wearing red shirts standing outside, guarding the path. Bobby recognized Harris right away.

"We're going back to our bunk," said Jessica. But as she tried to move past, the counselor grabbed her and threw her back into the mess hall.

Bobby jumped forward and grabbed the counselor by his throat. How dare he push Jessica. But *whack!* One of the red guards struck him across the back with a stick. He looked up just in time to see the fist of another red guard crash into his face. Blood immediately started pouring from his broken nose. Freddy tried to come to his aid but was also struck with a stick.

"Now, get the fuck back inside, Jew," screamed the red counselor. Harris, wearing his red shirt, looked on in horrified surprise.

"Stop!" he cried. "What the hell is wrong with you? This is just a game."

The counselor looked at him with disgust while raising his stick. "If you feel bad for these pigs you can sleep in the mess hall too. There are extra yellow shirts. That goes for all of you.

Anyone who disapproves of the treatment of the yellow team can join them."

Harris retreated. As they ganged up to push them back into the mess hall, Bobby could see Harris looking back at him and he seemed to mouth, "I'm sorry."

The door slammed shut and was locked from the outside.

Adam came over with some tissues and a bag of ice and tended to his nose. The other younger campers came over to see what had happened. Adam looked up and saw the worried looks on their faces. Some of the children were crying.

"Let's just play the game by their rules so no one else gets hurt. That goes for everyone here. If we behave and follow their rules, no one will get hurt. I'm sure the camp director will make sure we're treated fairly. Now try and get some sleep."

Fourteen

Auschwitz 1945

David, his mother, and his father took turns lying down in the dark train car against the wall. The car was actually meant for cattle. There were no seats and only one small barred window. They had been traveling for several days. There was no room in the car for everyone to sit or lie down. People were lying on top of each other, legs intertwined. It was the most horrific experience any of them had ever been a part of. There was no way of knowing but they estimated that there were sixty people crammed into the small space. The odor was worse than death. A mixture of body odor, vomit, and feces. Again, everyone shared a bucket that could be passed around. There was no paper or water to clean with. Another bucket was set down at each stop to be shared among them. This one was for drinking water. Bread was handed out as well. Some people developed dysentery and became severely dehydrated. A woman sitting next to David's family could not stop her diarrhea. She and his mom had been talking a little over the last couple of days. The woman, named Esther, said her husband, who had been carrying their son, got separated and was pushed onto the next train car. She had been holding her little girl's hand. Her sweet daughter Lena. Lena tripped, and she lost her grip on her little hand. An officer picked her up and carried her away. "I screamed at the top of my lungs and tried to fight my way to her, and then I was struck in the back of the head and woke up here next to you." Esther continued to weep as she told her story. The last thing she saw before blacking out was the officer putting Lena in the car behind her.

"What am I going to do? Oh God, if there is one, please keep my Lena safe. She's only six. Please help her be brave."

"If she is on the train behind us, then I'm sure you will be reunited with your family when we reach the camp," said Barbara as she put a gentle arm around the woman's shoulders.

Esther just stared ahead. The pain and worry were too much for her to bear. Over the rest of the day, Esther's sickness progressed. She had severe abdominal cramps, and she moaned, finally slipping out of consciousness. When the water bucket came around the next morning, Barbara tried to give the woman some, but she didn't respond. When she shook the woman, she felt cold to the touch, and it was clear that she was dead. For a moment Barbara thought to herself how lucky the dead lady was that her suffering had come to an end. But how devastated her husband and children would be. It hadn't occurred to her to ask her husband's name. How would he find out? At the next stop, her body along with those of two old men and a young boy who similarly perished the day before were removed from the train and tossed into the fields opposite the train station. In a sick way the remaining captives felt some relief that they now had a little more room to stretch out.

After what seemed like an eternity, the train reached its destination. The doors swung open. Nazi guards began to bark orders for everyone to get out. It was difficult to walk after being cramped in such tight quarters for so long. Men, women, and children tripped over each other as they disembarked the train. The officers yelled and beat the people who did not get up right away. Big German shepherds growled at the prisoners. An elderly man who was too weak to get up despite being motivated by the Nazi batons just lay down. After refusing to go on, an officer ordered his dog to attack. To David's horror, the dog lunged at the man, biting and tearing chunks of flesh from him as he screamed. Fredrick had seen enough. He jumped forward and kicked the dog hard in the side of its head. The dog, who did not see his foot coming, got knocked sideways. It was temporarily stunned and just lay there. David's father reached down to help the man to his feet. That was the last thing he ever did. A shot rang out and David watched in horror as his father collapsed on top of the man. The vicious attacks temporarily caused everyone in the immediate area to stop and just watch helplessly as Fredrick and the old man lay there in a bloody dead heap. Barbara shrieked and attempted to reach for her dead husband as the trooper raised his gun at her. David grabbed his mother and held her tightly. "Come on, Mama. Just close your eyes, please just close your eyes and breathe," he said.

"All right, back in line, keep moving," shouted an officer.

They walked forward in a daze. No one talked. Some sobbing could be heard from the frightened group. David and his mother were separated at the next checkpoint. Men on the right, women and children on the left. She walked away in a trance, saying nothing to David. She didn't even look back. David didn't know it at the time but that was the last time he would ever see her.

He would later find out that within an hour of arrival his mother had been sent to the gas chamber where she was asphyxiated. She was not alone. More than seventy-five percent of the new arrivals were executed as soon as they reached camp. They were deemed too unfit to work and so would be a waste of space and resources to feed and house. The odds of survival were even worse for the children. Not a single child under the age of twelve survived their first hour at the camp. Like David's mother, they were all gassed.

After being separated, the men were ushered into a large building, where they were ordered to strip and throw their dirty clothes in a pile in the corner that was already over ten feet high. They were marched naked in front of a brick wall. The normally humiliating condition of being forced to walk naked in front of the Nazi officers who were snickering and making fun of them didn't bother them in the slightest. The taunting was the least of David's problems. He was already dead inside after surviving that six-day train ride on the cattle car, watching his father get murdered, and being separated from his mother. Shockingly cold water seemed to burst out of nowhere, knocking some of the men off their feet.

The men were further separated into two lines. David was placed in a line with some of the older men. They crept along at a slow pace. The floor was cold and wet. The old man in front of him limped forward. His ankle, swollen and discolored, was clearly injured. His back was discolored as well with different shades of bruises that must have occurred during the journey. There were dark blue and purple marks along his buttocks. His upper back on the right side had a large area of a yellowish-green hue. His old skin hung loose and his back was crooked. He quietly moaned as he shuffled along. The man stepped forward into a large chamber. The room was dark and smelled of chemicals. David was about to step in as well when he heard, "Halt!"

He turned to the side and there, dressed sharply in his officer's uniform, was Eric. He looked David up and down, judging his appearance. Seeing Eric lifted his mood from despair to pure rage. He considered lunging at him and sinking his teeth into his neck but he needed to know if Emma and Otto were here and safe.

"Why is he in this line?" he shouted at the guards. "He is young and strong and fit for hard labor."

"Sorry, sir," said the closest guard. "I thought he looked like trouble so I sent him here."

"No, this prisoner will be my personal helper for the work I need done at my quarters. I'm building a six-foot brick wall around the property and need to have a play area constructed for my wife and son who joined me here just this week. Have him processed and then escort him to my quarters this evening for further instructions. And for God's sake, put some clothes on him. His parts remind me of a small boy." And with that he laughed sardonically, turned, and walked out.

David was issued a uniform. It was to be the only clothes he would have for the next two and a half years. At the next station he was assigned a number and it was branded upon his skin. He was assigned to building twelve. When he entered the barracks, he was immediately taken aback by the smell of unwashed skin, sweat, foul breath, urine, and feces all coming together into a dreadful odor of death. Each side of the building was lined with bunks. There were three levels. Three men were positioned on each level in an area designed to fit just one. For the lower and middle levels there was only enough space to lie down. It was impossible to sit up without hitting your head. David found a vacancy on a bottom bunk. There was a young man from Poland and his brother also lying in the space. They made room for him and tried to be pleasant but the language barrier made it impossible. In the back of the building were six seats with holes, which were the toilets. There were three on either side facing each other with no barriers for privacy.

David learned the routine fairly quickly. Each morning they would rise and go outside for roll call. After roll call, breakfast was handed out and usually consisted of watered-down soup. Sometimes they were fortunate enough to have a little piece of meat in the soup, but no one knew what kind of meat they were eating. And no one really cared either. Everyone was thin and wasted. Except for David, almost everyone looked like a skeleton. After breakfast, they would have to stand in line sometimes for hours waiting for their assignment. Those who spoke or were unable to stand in line were executed on the spot. Due to the poor nutrition and lack of hygiene, diarrhea was common. There was always a shortage of water, and what water they had was not clean. Out of thirst and a desire to go on, they drank the fetid water. A bathroom break was unacceptable during morning roll call. It could last hours, and if you had to move your bowels or urinate, your only choice was to go where you stood. This was particularly problematic as they never had a change of clothes. To solve this situation, they would sometimes use water from a nearby river when out on work duty to try and wash away the filth.

David's daily work was to tend and build things at Eric's house, right outside the gates of the main camp. On his first day at the camp, he was escorted to Eric's house. They met for the first time in private in what was to be the backyard of his house. David tried to look in the windows to see if he could catch a glimpse of Otto and Emma.

"Who are you looking for?" asked Eric. "Are you trying to see my wife and son? You know a man should not yearn for another man's family."

"That's my family, you sick monster! Eric, what happened to you? We have been best friends for as long as I can remember. We grew up together," David said.

"Then why did you try to steal Emma from me?"

"Eric, we both loved Emma. You went away, and we were left behind. We started a family. You were gone for years."

"I can forgive you for most things, David. You were a brother to me. It's only natural to have desired Emma. She is beautiful and loving. But why did you hide from me that you were a Jew? If you had told me, I could have helped you. But you lied to me. You didn't trust me," said Eric.

"How are Emma and Otto?" David asked, ignoring him.

"They're doing well. It's only been six days, but Otto is already calling me Papa. It's strange but I think he looks more like me than you."

"And Emma?"

"Well, she has been a bit tougher to tame. She seems to hate me. Of course, I have had to beat her on occasion."

"How could you, Eric?"

"Easy, easy. I have decided to look out for you. You know I'm not a monster. I have saved Emma and Otto from execution. If they knew that Emma had slept with a Jew, she would have been sentenced to death. No, Emma will be okay. I'm sorry for your situation, David. I'm so conflicted when it comes to you. To love a best friend, a cousin, as a brother, yet to find out he is a Jew. Well. I have saved your wife. I have saved your son. And I pulled you back from the brink of death. You will work here for me, and that will save you from hard labor. I will give you extra food when I can. You have nothing to fear for Emma and Otto. Otto is a happy little boy, and I will continue to satisfy Emma. I think she's actually beginning to enjoy making love to me."

David wanted to kill him then and there, but what could he do? This was an impossible situation. Eric had tortured his wife and claimed his son as his own, but without him, they would be dead. He had to give in.

"Eric, do you know where my mother is? Can I see her?"

"Oh yes, I was with her in line just before I came and rescued you," said Eric. "It was quite pitiful to see Aunt Barbara naked and in tears. She looked at me for a moment but didn't say anything. It was like her eyes were already dead. Of course, I could have helped her too. But her sin was worse than even yours or your father's. You two, while being unfortunately filthy Jews, did not choose to be that way. It is what you are, or were, in the case of your father." Eric laughed. "But your mother knew that your father was a Jew and married him anyway. Is there any worse kind of German? So, I let her walk into the gas chamber, where she died."

David felt like he could bear no more. Both of his parents had been executed today. His wife and son had been taken by another man. All he wanted at that moment was to die. But then he saw Emma's face in the corner of the window. Their eyes met. She looked so beautiful, despite her disheveled hair. It was clear that she was crying. There was a dark blue ring around her right eye.

David's face turned red with anger, and he balled his fists. "Did you hit her?" he screamed.

Eric turned to see Emma, who quickly ducked out of view below the windowsill. "David, you must learn to let go of your anger. It will do you no good. Emma was disobedient and I have to train her to be more docile. You know it gives me great pain to have to strike my wife. But don't worry, she is getting better."

David shouted, "She is my wife!"

"No! She is my wife. And if you know what's best for her and Otto you will forget that they were ever part of your life," said Eric. "Be back here tomorrow right after roll call. I have work for you to do. Dismissed!"

David turned, defeated, trying not to let Eric see the tears streaming down his face, and began walking back to his barracks.

"Oh, David, one more piece of news. I just got word today from the front. Your brother, Samuel, was exposed as a Jew. I'm told he wet his pants when they put the noose around his neck."

*

Over the years, David was able to get a glimpse of Emma and Otto in the window. Otto would wave to him, but it seemed more and more he was becoming a stranger to him. Emma would leave food wrapped in cloth outside where he was to work. It was this nutrition and the chance to see Emma every day that sustained him for nearly two and a half years at Auschwitz.

Everyone around David died. Numerous dead prisoners every morning would be collected after roll call. The bunk-mates would load their bodies on wagons and bring them to a large brick building with a smoke stack. Here they would be stripped and searched for any hidden possessions. Then they would be loaded on the rack and cremated. The crematorium seemed to smoke and send gray ash into the sky, where it would fall like rain, almost daily for the entire time David was there. New prisoners would constantly arrive, so the barracks never emptied. There was never room to get comfortable. Eventually, he grew accustomed to the smell and could sleep crammed next to the other sick, weak, and emaciated men. They never bathed. They never brushed their teeth.

David was never sure why Eric chose to spare him and even provide him with the comfort of working at his house instead of doing hard labor. He didn't think it was to make him envious. He thought that deep down, Eric was conflicted. On one hand, he was a cold-blooded Nazi killer who had executed his own parents, aunt, and uncle. He'd stolen his cousin and former best friend's wife and kid. But on the other hand, he seemed to feel some guilt, if only for David's situation. Even now, after all that had been done, it was because of Eric that David, Emma, and Otto still survived in relative comfort while thousands perished every day at the hands of the Nazis.

One afternoon in January of 1945, David was at Eric's house in the backyard fixing a broken piece of furniture. It was a cold winter. There was a light frost on the grass. He tried to keep moving to keep warm. He was lucky to have boots that Eric had left for him. Eric had gone out to survey the camp. All of a sudden, David felt a light hand on the back of his shoulder. He turned and looked up into the sun, and there was Emma. She pulled him quickly next to the house, and they bent down behind the adjacent shed.

"Emma, darling. Are you okay?" It was the first time they could speak since that night in Berlin.

She hugged him, but quickly withdrew. David didn't know if she was afraid they would get caught or if it was his physical condition and foul odor that caused her to pull back.

"David, quick, we have little time to talk. Eric is never gone for more than an hour. Tomorrow evening, he is planning a meeting with all of the guards and officials. I have heard him practicing his speech. The war effort is not going well for the Germans. The Russians apparently are moving in from the east, and the Americans from the west. I think we are only days away from the end. They are planning to destroy all of the documents and evidence of what has been going on here. Then they are planning to quickly execute all of the remaining prisoners and bury them in mass graves. It will take too long to cremate them all. They have been preparing for this eventuality. I'm told they have been taking prisoners out for several weeks into the forest to dig the massive holes.

They plan to shoot all of the Jews and bury them in the grave they have dug for themselves."

"Oh my God! I have to warn the other prisoners," whispered David as he tried to stand.

"Do it, but don't create a panic. They must plan for their own escapes. Tomorrow, come here right after eight p.m. Eric will have already left for the meeting. Otto and I will come out the back door, and we will escape in Eric's car. He keeps an extra gun in the glove box, which may come in handy. All of the guards except for a skeleton crew will be at the meeting. There are many empty homes in the surrounding forest. I've seen them with Eric. We will go and hide there and plan the rest of our escape."

"I don't know how to drive, Emma."

"Eric has taught me. I'm good at it now. I pretend I love him, and he treats us kindly. I'm sorry, David, but it has been the only way to protect Otto."

David looked away from Emma. He couldn't bear the thought of what she'd had to do to ensure their safety. How could she sleep with him and put on a smile, knowing that he had ordered the execution of her father?

"David, please. I know it's hard but I do it because we have no choice. Any other path leads to further misery and death. I couldn't let anything happen to you or Otto."

David looked back at her. She was so beautiful and brave. He leaned in and kissed her gently. She didn't pull away. She held him for a moment and then said, "Tomorrow at eight p.m. Don't be late." She got up to run back inside.

"Wait, Emma. Tell me about Otto."

"Otto is a good boy. He's almost six years old. He is

healthy, tall, and thin. He looks like you when you were about his age. David, I'm sorry but he thinks Eric is his father. It's for the best for now. It's the only way I can protect him."

Hearing this, David felt a sharp pain in his chest. His little boy didn't know him anymore. Emma, sensing his thoughts, reassured him, "It's only temporary. He will be your son again. It's not too late for that. Tomorrow night our life starts again. I must go back. If Eric catches me our plans will be ruined." She ran inside, closing and locking the door behind her.

David lay in bed that night, thinking through the plan. He had a permanent pass to go through the main gates any time of day and walk straight to Eric's house. That part would be easy. From Eric's house, there would still be one more gate as they exited toward the forest. There would be at least two guards there. But it would be dark, and they would be in Eric's car. Perhaps that would be enough to pass by. If worse came to worse and they were stopped, maybe David would be able to shoot the men with Eric's gun. If he fired the gun, though, would that alert other guards to what was going on? Gunshots were a regular thing in camp as prisoners were always being executed at all hours. And then, if they were lucky enough to escape, what would they do for food? How could he protect Emma and Otto? One thing was for sure. No matter how dangerous the plan was, staying was even more dangerous. David would likely be killed and buried in a mass grave, and Eric would run off with Emma and Otto. At least they would be safe with Eric. But he was a madman, and in the end, they could never really be safe with him. David decided to go through with Emma's plan.

He began to whisper among the other prisoners what was

planned for them. The news spread from camper to camper. Men quietly talked about possible solutions. Should they try to fight back? They were all so weak. Most of them looked like skeletons. There was no chance of fighting. They could try to delay by working slowly, but that would only lead to their execution. Ultimately, their best hope was to be liberated by the Americans or the Russians.

Some commotion was heard from the other barracks as men and women were ordered out of bed and to begin marching. David wondered where they were going. Were they going to dig that mass grave now? At night? He had never seen so many prisoners marched out of camp at one time. There didn't seem to be enough guards for all of them. He wondered why their barracks were left alone. Why didn't they have to dig? Maybe they didn't have enough guards to support such a huge group outside the gates. They all discussed it late into the night and finally went to sleep filled with worry. For the first time in a long time, David also had the faintest bit of hope for a possible new life with Emma and Otto.

David woke the next morning to the sound of large trucks driving through the camp. Walking outside, prisoners were just milling around, watching as Russian soldiers drove through and inspected the camps. All of the German soldiers were gone. There were no guards at their posts or in the towers. Most of the camp was empty. With the help of some Red Cross members traveling alongside the army, food was being handed out by the Russian soldiers. The newly freed prisoners looked around in disbelief. What should they do now? They were so used to their routine that some were even still lining up for roll call. No one was cheering. There was no real celebration. The day they had been praying for had come. This marked the end of the death camp and the beginning of the rest of their life. However, none of them would ever live a normal life. Most of the lucky few who survived had likely already lost their spouse, parents, and children. David had lost his mother, father, brother, aunt and uncle during the war. His story was not uncommon. Those were just five of the over ten million people that had been murdered by the Nazis.

Apparently, the evening before, the vast majority of the camp had been forced to leave, and the prisoners were marched toward trains where they were to be transported to other camps deeper in Germany. David spoke with one of the Red Cross personnel who asked about their treatment. The Russian soldiers, known for their brutality, could not believe the condition of the prisoners. They could not believe that women and children were executed in cold blood. Years later, David would find out that 1.3 million men, women, and children passed through the gates of Auschwitz, of which 1.1 million died of execution, disease, human experimentation, and starvation.

After the shock of the liberation wore off, David's attention immediately turned to Emma and Otto. Would they have been mistaken for Nazis and killed by the Russians? Sprinting through the camp, David passed through the now unguarded gate and toward Eric's house. No one seemed to be there. He tried the front door, which was locked. Then he moved around to the back and saw that one of the windows by the kitchen was slightly open. He pushed it up. "Emma! Otto!" he screamed. He climbed up through the window and into the house. Running through the rooms, it looked like they had evacuated in a hurry. There were no clothes in the master bedroom. The dresser drawers had been left open, and some were taken out and placed on the floor in a heap. He went into a smaller bedroom. Lying on the bed was a worn stuffed animal. David remembered that toy. Otto had always kept it with him. He used to sleep with it tucked in his arms every night. Picking up the stuffed animal, he ran out the back door, and to his dismay, the car was gone. Emma, Otto, and Eric had disappeared.

Fifteen

Camp Ohiwa 1965

Four days after the beginning of "guards versus prisoners," the campers were lined up at the crack of dawn. They were getting used to the daily routine. They would wake up at six a.m. and line up for roll call. At roll call, they wouldn't answer by their names but by their numbers. Eric, who was now the "Camp Commandant" instead of the camp director, had the idea to write a number on the back of each yellow prisoner's neck. This number was their identifier. They were not allowed to call each other by name. They were not allowed to wear anything but the same yellow shirt each day. When rules were broken, they could be hit with a wooden stick right there in front of everyone else, or sometimes the offender would be taken into bunk six, which was repurposed as the punishment room. After the first night sleeping in the mess hall, they were allowed to return to the bunks, but all thirty of the yellow team boys were in one bunk and the girls were in another bunk. The red team had put fifteen beds in each bunk, meaning that they had to share twin beds with another camper. The overcrowding in the small bunks in the hot summer without air conditioning resulted in stinky conditions. The hot bunk smelled of unwashed feet and armpits. They didn't have access to their toothbrushes, and there was no soap in the showers. Worse than that, there was no toilet paper. When they complained, they were punished. They tried to coordinate so that one older boy and one younger boy would share each cot, as it was impossible to fit two teenage boys in a single bed. Bobby shared his bed with a ten-year-old named Dylan. They decided they would get more sleep if one started on the floor and then switched halfway through the night. Bobby would usually lie on the floor next to Freddy, and then around midnight, they would get up and lift the younger boys onto the ground and take their place in the beds. It was hot, and it was gross.

On each day, the conditions seemed to become worse. The red guards grew meaner. They would become more physically and verbally abusive. Some of them would spit in their faces. If they fought back the penalty would be severe. On the third day after roll call, they were meant to do chores at the request of the red team. Marvin and Bobby were assigned to cleaning bunk seven, which was a red team bunk. There were just six beds in the bunk. They were told to collect the laundry and bring it to the laundry room, which was worked by other yellow campers. Bobby thought they deliberately left their clothes in a mess so that they would be humiliated in collecting it. There were dirty socks and underwear strewn across the floor. After dropping off the laundry, Bobby and Marvin returned to make the beds, sweep, and mop the floors and then clean the showers and toilets. After their work was done, Eric, Otto, and a group of red campers came through to inspect the work. Marvin and Bobby stood at attention.

"Prisoner 00016 and prisoner 00037," said Eric as he walked on by. Those were the numbers that had been assigned to them and written on the back of their necks. "What do you have to say for yourselves?"

"Sir?" Bobby asked, not knowing what he was looking for.

"You were instructed to clean this bunk and yet it is still filthy."

"Are you kidding?" cried Marvin. Bobby looked at him, surprised by his audacity. Apparently, Eric was surprised as well because he stepped forward, towering over Marvin, looking him directly in the eye.

"Repeat yourself, 00037!"

"Eric, this is getting out of hand. This is abuse, and I want to call my parents and go home," responded Marvin, looking up at him but holding his gaze as long as he dared.

"And why should I listen to a filthy Jew?" said Eric.

"When my parents find out what your—"

But Marvin was cut off by a quick punch to the gut, dropping him to his knees. He was on the floor gasping for air with the wind apparently knocked out of him. Otto came forward, putting a hand on his father, as though afraid that he would strike the boy again. But Eric brushed him off and glared at him. Otto backed down.

"Guards, take prisoner 00037 to the punishment bunk. It appears he has not yet learned his place."

The red guards picked up Marvin by both arms and began to lead him out of the bunk.

"Halt! I've changed my mind. I think we will make an

example of him in case anyone else believes that this is just a game. Strip him to his underwear and tie him to the flagpole. When he is ready, sound the assembly."

"Please, no, no!" pleaded Marvin, with tears coming down his face.

"Too late for that, Jew. Take him away!"

Fifteen minutes later, the yellow campers were lined up at assembly. The red campers were lined up at their posts on the group's perimeter. Their familiar and frequent chant grew louder and louder.

"Beware of the crooked
Beware of the Jew
Cover your belongings
Or they will steal from you!
Go Red, Go Red
If they won't stop, make them dead!

"Beware of the crooked
Beware of the Jew
Cover your belongings
Or they will steal from you!
Go Red, Go Red.
If they won't stop, make them dead!"

The yellow children stared in horror at the sight of fifteen-year-old Marvin tied to the flagpole with his hands strapped behind him, wearing only his underwear. His face was dirty, and tears were falling down his cheeks, making brown streaks. Marvin had tried to hold it together, but now he was afraid and humiliated. The red campers pointed and snickered at him. Some of the girls blushed and laughed and whispered in each other's ears. Some of the red shirts, including Harris, just stared into the ground.

The crowd quieted as Eric walked to the center and stood towering over the weeping boy tied to the pole.

"Here at camp, we have rules that are meant to ensure order and good behavior. The rules are simple, and as long as you follow the rules, we can all live in harmony. However, it is now plain to see what I have known all of my life: Jews cannot be trusted. Prisoner 00037 committed a heinous crime, and he will have to be punished. Part of the punishment is the humiliation he now suffers as you look at his scrawny body and dirty underwear. You can see he lacks any muscle or any other signs of being a man, yet he disrespects men as if he were a strong man himself. Now, as his punishment, each of you yellow shirts will take a turn throwing a tennis ball at him from a distance of fifteen feet. If you miss or if you intentionally throw the ball weakly, you will be required to do thirty pushups and will be docked tonight's dinner. Now line up at the marker that Otto has placed in front of prisoner 00037."

The prisoners lined up as instructed. One by one they took their turn throwing the tennis ball at Marvin. Many of the campers missed and were roughly pushed to the field to begin their pushups. Many hit their mark. Luckily no one hit him in his face or his private parts. When Bobby got to the front of the line, he stared Marvin in the eyes. He would have missed on purpose, for the pushups were not a hardship for him, but he was starving. For the past three days, they had been given just two small meals per day. In the morning, they had a bread roll, and in the evening, they would get another bread roll and a cup of soup. Crying, Bobby reached back and threw the ball, which hit Marvin on the right side of the chest. He grunted. Bobby mouthed, "I'm sorry," as tears began to fall down his face. This torture continued for the better part of ten minutes. Toward the end of the line, a young girl with blonde hair came to the front. Bobby didn't know her name, but she appeared to be about nine years old. She was handed a ball but just dropped it. Two red guards, each about fourteen, yelled at her to pick it up.

"Pick it up, prisoner 00002."

"No!" she cried.

"You will pick it up or else."

"No! This is mean, and it's not fair. No one here has the right to hurt him. You have to untie him now."

"Throw the ball now, prisoner 00002," shouted Eric, now walking over.

"No, you are a horrible man, and so are all of you reds who just follow him." She picked up the ball and, from two feet away, threw it at one of the red guards, striking him in the nose.

He was shocked at first, then reached up to touch his face. When he looked down at his hand, he was further shocked to see blood. His face turned red, and he narrowed his eyes. In the blink of an eye, he picked up his stick and smashed it across the back of the girl's head, dropping her instantly to the ground. Her body convulsed with her legs jerking several times back and forth. And then she lay motionless. There was absolute silence.

Otto ran over and pushed the guards back so that he could see the little girl on the ground. She had fallen face down. Her blond hair was soaked with bright red blood. He turned her over, and she just stared back at him. Not breathing. Otto checked her pulse and found none. She had been killed instantly by the devastating blow to the back of her head. Otto looked up at the red guards in horror.

"We need an ambulance. Father, quick, call for an ambulance!"

The boys in the red shirts stepped back, horror washing over their faces. Dawn, in her red shirt, came running over. She gasped as she knelt down next to the little girl. She picked her up, rocking her little body, tears streaming down her face.

"Put her down. She is dead," said Eric in a stern and cold tone. "An ambulance will do her no good."

Turning to the red guards, he ordered them to move her body out of the sun and into the camp office.

"Pick two Jews to dig a grave for her and bury her there with haste," he continued.

Dawn, still kneeling on the ground holding the little girl's body, looked up at Eric defiantly and said, "No! Enough is enough. This has gone too far. We must call the police and her parents."

Eric, ignoring her, repeated his instruction to take the girl away. When Dawn refused to give in, Eric gave her a backhand slap across the face and lifted her by her hair. Freddy jumped forward to help Dawn but was quickly grabbed by the red guards. "Otto, take her to the punishment bunk. Give her a yellow shirt to wear. This goes for all of you. If you sympathize with the prisoners, you will become one yourself. No exceptions. Take him too," Eric said, pointing at Freddy. "I will decide their fate later. No dinner tonight for them. Tomorrow, I think I will have them tied to the pole and punished."

The guards led Dawn and Freddy to the punishment bunk. Bobby needed to help Freddy, but he was powerless to do so. Any more resistance would lead to further cruelty or get them killed. Looking around, he could see that some of the red guards were uncomfortable with what was happening, but even more seemed to be enjoying their positions of power.

Jonathan, Jessica, and Bobby milled around outside the bunks waiting for dinner to be served. Harris, in his red shirt, walked by and stopped, pretending to be patrolling and looking the other way.

"Harris," Bobby said. "You have to help us. We need to free Freddy and Dawn."

"Even if I could help you get them out of the punishment bunk, what would you do then?" he asked, not looking in their direction.

"I don't know. Maybe we could make a run for it. Try to get help at one of the other camps on the other side of the lake."

"Eric has guards posted on all of the exits and trails leading away."

"Could we fight our way through?" Bobby asked.

"Maybe, but you would have to be quick. If they alert Eric of your escape, he will hunt you down, and then who knows what he will do. He didn't even flinch when they killed that girl today."

A feeling of shame went through Bobby at the mention

of the little girl. He didn't even know her name. He was only concerned with his own survival and that of his brother and friends. He thought for a moment about the girl's parents. What would they do when they found out their daughter was murdered at sleepaway camp? It was supposed to be a safe place for kids to grow and have fun and gain independence. It made him sick and he tried to push the thought from his mind.

"Harris, can you get us into Eric's office so we can call for help?"

"He has two boys standing guard out front all day and night. You might be able to sneak in through the window in the back by his office. His bedroom is upstairs. Otto also has a room upstairs."

Jessica, Jonathan, and Bobby began to formulate a plan. They needed to get help before the morning. Before Freddy and Dawn were marched out to be humiliated and punished in who knew what cruel way. That night, Bobby would slip out of the bunk by way of the window in the back by the bathrooms. There were definitely guards at the entrance of the boys' and girls' bunks. Jessica would create a distraction by opening the door to the girls' bunk at the same time and ask for medical attention. Jonathan would also slip out the window with Bobby. Bobby was going to work his way to the camp office, get in through the window, and call for help. Jonathan would try to quietly make it through the woods down to the lake and then hike to one of the camps on the other side of the lake and try to get help there. Once the ruse was up with Jessica, she would meet them down by the boat house, where they would wait for help. Jonathan and Bobby would slip out of the bunk at midnight. Jessica would open the front door and ask for help at that exact time.

As Bobby lay there in his bunk watching the clock, he reflected on the situation. It was unbelievable to think that in just a matter of days, under the leadership of one deranged man, one group of people could turn on another so quickly. Friends of many years had turned on each other overnight. Some did so out of fear, but others enjoyed the change. It was also unbelievable that the yellow group so easily accepted their roles as prisoners and didn't resist with any strength. This seemed impossible. But he knew it wasn't. While his father never talked of the war, he knew about the history of Germany. He was well aware of the Nazis and their treatment of the Jews. He knew about the unthinkable atrocities of the Holocaust. That happened on a much more grand and sinister scale. But they were just kids.

It was hot, and they were hungry and tired. Looking around the bunk, he could see that everyone was asleep. Some on the floor and some on the beds. At 11:58, Jonathan and Bobby slowly got off the beds and crept past the sleeping children toward the back of the bunks. The floorboards creaked, but no one stirred. The light was always on in the bathroom, making it easy to find their way. Bobby opened the window all of the way and climbed up and jumped out, landing as quietly as possible on the dirt and leaves outside. Jonathan quickly followed. They crouched there for a moment, waiting for Jessica to make her move.

A short scream came from the girls' bunk, and a moment later, they could hear the door to the bunk open. Jessica had cut her leg with a razor to create a scene that would distract the guards, and it worked. There was a commotion as the guards from the boys' and girls' bunks ran to see what was going on. At that moment, Jonathan and Bobby ran out from behind the bunks. Bobby went in the direction of the camp office while Jonathan made his way to the lake.

The camp was mostly dark at night. There were a few spotlights up on the trees that illuminated some of the paths. Also, there was a light above the doors of each bunk and camp building. It was a warm night, and the ground was damp. Bobby crept along the path, careful to avoid the lights. Except for a few red guards on duty, most of the children were asleep. After making his way behind each bunk to the end of the buildings, he arrived at a grassy field that he needed to cross before getting under the cover of the trees again. He could then cut through the trees off the path past the mess hall to where the camp director's office was. He silently made his way across the field and then slowly through the trees. He paused at the edge of the trees and could now make out the director's office with the two red guards stationed out front on rocking chairs. Unfortunately, it was Luke and Peter, who were sixteen-year-old boys that had really seemed to enjoy their role as red team guards. Luke was a pimply-faced kid who was always more on the quiet side but had seemed to become louder and braver in his new role. Peter was a muscular boy, tan, with blond hair. He was known for being a great athlete. He also seemed to enjoy the cruelty of his new role. They were quietly talking to each other, about what Bobby couldn't hear. He moved stealthily through the shadows toward the back of the house, staying at least fifty feet away until he was out of their line of sight.

Thankfully, the back window was open as usual. The lights were off downstairs, but one of the lights upstairs was on. It could have been Eric's or Otto's room. All was quiet. The wood protested as Bobby lifted the window higher to make room for him to crawl through. He pushed as slowly as he could, but it was impossible to do it in silence. He waited a few minutes, and not hearing any stirring in the house, he lifted his body through the window and put his right foot down on the floor. He was almost in when his left foot knocked over a vase sitting on a small table below the window. In slow motion, he saw it falling to the floor. It would surely sound the alarm, and he would be caught, but he reached it just in time with his right hand. He carefully settled it down and then tiptoed across to Eric's desk.

Picking up the phone receiver, he realized that he didn't know the number for the local police station. The room was too dark, and he couldn't see a phone directory. The only thing to do was to call his parents. He dialed the number and the phone began to ring. It rang three, four times. Bobby's shirt was soaked with perspiration. He tried to calm his breathing. *Come on, pick up, pick up.* Finally, on the fifth ring, his mom answered.

"Hello?" she said in a sleepy voice. "Who is it?"

"Mom, it's me," he whispered. "Bobby."

"Bobby? What time is it? Are you okay?"

"Mom, I need help. Is Dad there?"

"What's wrong, baby? David, wake up. Bobby's on the phone."

"Bobby, what's happening? Are you okay?" asked his father, still not fully awake.

"Dad, please help us!" He started crying. Bobby didn't realize how terrible and scared he felt until he tried to explain what was going on to his dad.

"Bobby, Bobby, what is it?" he asked.

"Dad, it's terrible. They have made all the Jews prisoners here, and they killed this little girl. I think they're going to kill us too. They locked up Freddy. Help us, please."

"What? Who did this? Killed? What's going on?"

"Please just help us."

There was the sound of a toilet flushing. Then footsteps from the second floor and a door opening. The footsteps were now coming from the stairs.

"Hurry, Dad! I have to go."

"Bobby, Bobby!"

Click. Bobby had to hang up. He quickly climbed up and through the window, carefully avoiding the vase. He didn't have time to close the window because just as he hit the ground, the door to the office opened, and a light was switched on. He crouched behind a tree. There standing in the window looking out was Eric. He seemed to look right at Bobby, but the light in the room must have blinded him to his presence. He was about to get up when the phone rang. Eric spun around, clearly surprised to hear the camp phone ringing at this time of night.

"Hello?" he said. "This is the camp director." *Pause.* "Mr. Grossbaum? Who did you say called you?" *Pause.* "He said what?" *Pause.* "Oh, what an imagination these kids have. No, no, the children are having a lovely time. We had color wars last week. Your boys are great athletes and have had the time of their lives." *Pause.* "No, I can't believe he said that to you.

You know the boys have been playing this dare game with each other where they have been making up pranks, and some have called their parents with these jokes." *Pause.* "No, wow, what an imagination. I agree that is a terrible thing to say. I have to say Bobby took this prank a little too far. I will speak with him in the morning and have him call you. Yes, yes. Don't worry. Get some rest. I will have both of your boys call you in the morning."

Eric unhooked the phone and took it with him as he called for Otto and then marched out the front door.

"Luke, Peter! Let's go. Otto, sound the assembly. I want all the Jews to line up. I think some have been up to no good."

Sixteen

Camp Ohiwa 1965

A police patrol car came through the camp gates around an hour and a half later and stopped in front of the camp director's office. All was quiet at the camp. Two officers got out of the car and, using flashlights, approached the front door. They knocked several times before finally a light went on upstairs. After a few moments, Eric opened the door. His hair was disheveled, and he looked as if he'd just woken up from a deep sleep.

"Officers, what has happened?" he said.

"We are responding to a call from David Grossbaum, who said he received a call about someone being held prisoner here."

"Prisoner?" asked Eric, feigning surprise.

"The caller was frantic, saying that there were children being murdered."

"Dear God!" exclaimed Eric. "Some of these boys have been making prank calls to their parents as some sort of game, but this has gone too far. Oh, I imagine the poor parents must be beside themselves. I will need to put a stop to this behavior right away. I'm so sorry to have troubled you, officers."

"You don't mind if we take a look around the camp and see for ourselves, do you?" asked the officer.

"No, of course not. It's dark though. Let me put on my shoes, and I can show you around."

"We would like to see the boy who made the call as well, uh, a Bobby Grossbaum."

"Yes, yes. I will take you to his bunk. Let me just check the roster to see which one he is in."

Eric stepped back into the house for a minute, then returned with a flashlight and led the officers to the bunks.

Ninety minutes earlier, Eric had awakened all of the children and had them stand in line for roll call. The sleepy children cowered outside while the red guards accounted for the prisoners. Eric paced up and down the lines, baton in hand, looking even more fierce than usual. Otto reported that in addition to the two children in the punishment bunk, three more were missing. Eric sent out three teams of four guards to search for the missing kids.

"To be extra safe, move all of the Jews to the barn on the far side of the soccer field. Lock them in there for the night. I think we may be getting some visitors tonight. Once you have secured the Jews, bring the red team back to their bunks to sleep. I need all of the red team sleeping in their own beds tonight. You go stay with the kids in the punishment bunk and keep them quiet by any means necessary."

Otto led the Jews to the barn as instructed. A few minutes later, eight red shirts came up the path and onto the field in front of where Eric was standing. Bobby and Jessica were with them. Tears were running down both their dirt-stained faces. Their hands were tied behind their backs. Jessica was clearly in tremendous pain. She had blood running down her leg. Her arm appeared raw, swollen, and exquisitely tender.

"We found them down by the boat house. A third one—Jonathan, uh, I mean prisoner 00022—was dead. He must have hit his head on the rocks trying to escape. We tied some rocks around him and pushed him into the lake. He went down like an anchor," the boy laughed.

The laughing was too much for Jessica who began sobbing uncontrollably. This was all too overwhelming. Eric hit her in the stomach with a baton, which doubled her over and temporarily stopped her crying while she tried to catch her breath.

Eric turned his attention back to the guards. "Well done. Take them to Otto in the punishment bunk and then return to bed. You can all have the rest of the night off."

"You will never get away with this, monster. The police are coming," screamed Bobby.

"I don't think so," said Eric. "If by some chance we do get visitors tonight, Luke, you will say you're Freddy, and Peter, you will be Bobby."

"Yes, sir!" they shouted.

In the punishment bunk, they tied Bobby and Jessica to the beds next to where Freddy and Dawn were being held. All four had their mouths duct-taped shut.

Ninety minutes later, Eric led the police officers past the mess hall, athletic fields, and rifle range. The police did a brief search and saw that everything was quiet and in order. They then went up to the bunks, and Eric led the officers inside, where they quietly looked at the sleeping children in their red shirts. They moved through each bunk before coming to the one where Luke and Peter were feigning sleep.

"Officers, did you want to see Bobby and Freddy?" whispered Eric.

"Yes," they replied.

Eric reached down and shook Luke and Peter by their feet. They pretended to be startled.

"Freddy, Bobby, get up. The police have some questions for you." The boys climbed out of bed and followed Eric and the officers outside.

"Who is Bobby?" one officer asked.

"I am, sir," said Peter.

"I understand you wanted to report a murder and some prisoners being held against their will?"

Peter looked down, feigning shame, and said, "Sorry, officer, it was just a prank. We dared each other to call our parents. It was just a joke."

"That is some joke. You know there are consequences for this kind of behavior. You caused your parents to panic and took two busy police officers away from our other duties. This does not seem like a very funny joke. Maybe we should take you down to the precinct and charge you with a crime."

"Please, officers, I'm so sorry. I never knew a prank could cause this much trouble."

Eric stepped in. "Officers, we have strict protocols about behavior here, and these boys will likely be expelled in the morning. Allow me to handle it, please."

"Very well, this camp has a great reputation. Just keep your campers in line. Now show us back to our car."

They started to walk back toward the car when one officer asked who was in the bunks on the other side. They were pointing to some empty bunks as well as the one reserved for punishment.

"They are only used in July when the camp is full. Many of our children go home after four weeks, and we shut down the bunks on that side," explained Eric.

"Okay, director. We'll be on our way."

The three men walked back to the office, where the police got in the car, and Eric watched as they drove off.

Seventeen

Camp Ohiwa 1965

They had moved the four prisoners to chairs in the dimly lit bunk. Their hands were tied behind their backs and they had duct tape covering their mouths. Jessica looked the worst. She was sweating profusely. There was blood covering much of her leg, although it was no longer bleeding. Her face was contorted in pain, and it was clear her arm was broken. Bobby was relieved to see Freddy and Dawn looked relatively uninjured. Four of the red guards stood around glaring at them, waiting for instructions. Otto paced the floor, looking anxious.

The door opened, and Eric walked in. The red guards snapped to attention.

"Well done!" said Eric, looking at Otto. "The police are gone."

"Father, this game has gotten out of control. It's gone too far," said Otto.

"This is not a game. We are resuming our work. The Jews have forgotten their place. It's like nothing ever happened. They are back controlling banks and politics. Meanwhile,

Germany has been humiliated. The Jews set the whole thing up."

"But Dad, the war is over. Everyone knows Adolf Hitler was a madman. He put millions of innocent Jews, gypsies, and political enemies to death. Even children."

"Innocent. Ha. And don't even bring up Hitler's name. He was a failure. Had he been stronger we wouldn't be in this mess."

"What mess?" asked Otto.

"Otto, you are weak and disappoint me. You remind me of your mother. She never fully embraced the work we did. To think I raised you as my own."

"What are you saying?"

"You are weak and a lousy excuse for a son. Get out of my sight."

"What are you planning, Father?" asked Otto.

"Get out of here before I bind you to a chair as well," said Eric, spittle coming out of his mouth. He took a step toward Otto, raising his baton.

Otto turned and ran out of the bunk.

Eric began to pace up and down in front of the four bound friends. He was heated now, and his eyes looked crazed. He took his baton and pressed it to Bobby's chin, pushing it up. Bobby squirmed but was unable to move. Eric pulled a knife from his belt with his other hand and put the point of it against Bobby's throat. Freddy tried in vain to wriggle loose from the rope.

Eric was enjoying himself now. Walking from one child to the next, taunting them with the blade. He drew superficial blood but was content to take his time. He hadn't noticed that the four red guards were still standing at attention until now and finally turned and dismissed them.

"I will punish these four by myself. Go get some sleep. We have much to do in the morning," he said.

Without another word, they filed out of the bunk.

"I have a confession to make," said Eric. "I'm not really an experienced camp director. I did, however, help run one of the most famous concentration camps in Poland during the war. I helped exterminate over one million Jews, including men, women, and children, during my time there. I also rid Germany of non-Jewish traitors like you, Dawn. I look back with sadness that I couldn't finish the job that Hitler had set off to do. At dawn, I plan to set fire to the athletic barn and do my small part to rid the world of you roaches. Oh, I know you cannot be fully exterminated. Like roaches, a few of you will always escape. In just a couple of hours, though, I will burn alive the remaining Jewish children and do my small part to create a better future."

The four children continued to struggle against the bonds holding them to the chairs, crying inaudibly against the duct tape.

"Don't worry, you won't have to be there to hear the children scream or smell the burning flesh because I am going to cut your throats now. Before I do, I have one last confession to make. You see, after the war I was forced to flee. All of the cowards ran into hiding and the world despicably changed sides. Now suddenly the villainous Jews were looked at with compassion and we Nazis who had done all of the hard work had to run with our tail between our legs. I moved around a lot after the war, dragging my family from country to country, changing our names. Finally, we settled in a sleepy town in New Jersey not too far from New York City. One day, I was walking through the grocery store when I thought I saw a ghost. I saw my long-lost cousin for the first time since the war sorting through some oranges in the fruit section. I thought he had died during the war but there he was. I followed him home. I was surprised to see he had married and had two sons. Bobby and Freddy, I knew your dad. You see, he is my cousin, and at one time we were best friends. We grew up together. Your father hid the fact that he was half Jewish from me. The betrayal almost cost me my career. Then he stole my wife and got her pregnant and had a little boy named Otto. It was this incredible betrayal that led to the death of my parents and your grandparents as well. Your cowardly grandmother and grandfather marched to their deaths at Auschwitz without a fight. Typical cowardly Jews."

Eric was no longer looking crazed but seemed to be taking comfort in hearing himself retell the story.

"I righted the wrong, of course. I took my wife back and took Otto as well. He was just three years old at the time. I see now that the Jewish blood that courses through his veins has made him weak. I tried to raise him as a proper German, but I failed in this. He is weak like his father, David. Think about your father. You must be disgusted to hear that a grown man could give up his wife and son at gunpoint. Your father was more concerned about his own safety than his wife and child. It makes you think. What would he do now to save you if he could? You may think he would risk his neck for you but I have seen it with my own eyes. The coward wouldn't pull a hair for you."

After a pause, Eric continued. "Now that you know, it's time to say goodbye. Let's see whose neck I will cut first."

He started with Bobby and moved down the line. "Eenie, meenie, miney, moe, catch the Jew by his toe, if he hollers cut his throat, eenie, meenie, miney, moe."

He put his knife to Freddy's throat and was about to slice into his skin when the door burst open. A man in his mid-forties charged through.

"Stop!" he shouted. The man looked from one child to the next and his heart stopped as he saw a man with a knife to Freddy's neck.

"What the hell is going on? Take that knife off my son's neck or I will separate your head from your shoulders."

Eric looked up, initially shocked by the intrusion, but he quickly regained his composure.

"David, my old friend. You have grown old and fat."

David, stunned by the sight of the man standing before him, felt his knees go weak and grabbed the door to steady himself.

"Eric, you survived? What are you doing here? Get away from my boys. Haven't you caused enough misery?"

Eric began to laugh. "Oh, you haven't seen anything yet. You have never fully paid for your betrayal."

"*My* betrayal? You turned me in to the Gestapo. You had my mother and father killed. You sent word of my brother's true identity and he was killed as well. You executed your own family, and you stole my wife and son! We were cousins and best friends since boyhood, and you destroyed me," cried David.

"You are a twisted Jew. You distort the truth to serve your

own purposes. It was you who hid your identity from me. It was you who stole Emma from me. And it was you that drove her to madness," said Eric.

David, feeling the strength returning to his legs, took a step toward Eric and the four children. He looked at Bobby and Freddy tied to the chairs and the bloody visions from Auschwitz returned to him. They were so frightened.

"I'm going to untie the children. We're leaving," said David.

"Not another step," said Eric as he pushed the knife harder against Freddy's neck, drawing some blood and a muffled shriek from David's son.

"Eric, please. The war is over. There is nothing left to fight for. Please don't hurt the kids. They are innocent."

"Pfft. Your blood courses through their veins. How right I would be to take their lives now so you can see what it feels like to have someone stolen from you," said Eric.

"Eric, I didn't steal anyone from you. Emma was never yours to keep."

"You never learn. She was mine. You were my cousin and best friend, and you married my girl. You stabbed me in the back. I'm sorry, David, but nothing would give me more pleasure than having you watch as I stab young Freddy in the back." Eric moved the knife away from Freddy's throat and pushed it hard into the right side of his upper back. Freddy convulsed in pain. Blood almost immediately started to come up through his nose, and he turned blue as he began to choke on his own blood.

David stared in horror but only for a moment. His fear and sorrow turned to rage as he lunged at Eric, grabbing him by the neck and knocking over Dawn's chair in the process.

Eric hit the back of his head on the wood floor as he fell to the ground, temporarily stunning him. David straddled Eric and punched him in the face one, two, three times. Blood spurted from his mouth and nose, splattering up onto David's face. He reached down to choke his cousin as Eric's eyes stared right back, still glazed over from the fall. But the blood-gurgling sound coming from Freddy brought David back from his rage. Quickly getting up, he ran to Freddy and ripped the duct tape from his mouth. Freddy spit out a mouthful of blood as he gasped for air. He was still bleeding but not as profusely. He looked pale and sweaty. "Freddy, are you okay?" he asked.

"I-I feel weak and dizzy, Dad," said Freddy.

"Come on, let's get you some help." David looked up at Bobby and the two girls tied to their chairs, the duct tape smothering their sobs. "Let me untie the others, and then—"

Thwack.

That was the last David heard. He woke up a few minutes later. His head was throbbing, and he didn't recognize his surroundings at first. He tried to get up but was now tied to a chair. Eric had smashed him over the back of the head, knocking him out. He'd tied him up and put the four children back in line on the chairs. He reapplied the duct tape to Freddy's mouth, who was now slouching over, barely conscious, and breathing awkwardly through his nose. For the first time, he had a clear view of the other children. They were dirty and disheveled, with a look that he hadn't seen in about twenty years. They did not look afraid but defeated. They were resigned to their fate. It was an expression he recognized from the other prisoners from his time at Auschwitz.

He looked up at Eric, who was standing there tall and strong, his cold blue eyes staring back at him.

"It's over, David. I have always bested you, and today is more of the same. Today I will finally kill you. But not before I mutilate your children before cutting their throats. And then when you can bear to watch no more and have lost everything, I will give you mercy and separate your head from your shoulders."

"You have already taken everything from me, Eric. You killed me twenty years ago when you took my Emma and Otto and killed my entire family. You have already won. Please spare the children. Kill me, then cut them free. Let them go," pleaded David.

Eric moved over to David and taped his mouth shut as well. "Now enjoy the show."

Eric took a step toward Bobby. He withdrew his knife and pointed it at his neck. He turned to look at David. A crazed look came over his face. "This is for—"

Suddenly blood shot down across Bobby's face as Otto's knife plunged through the back of Eric's neck and out the front. Eric briefly coughed and gasped for air as blood gushed from his throat before collapsing on top of Bobby.

Eighteen

New Jersey 1965

David and Otto were driving along Route 4 toward the Worthington Psychiatric Unit in Northern NJ. Otto was sitting in the passenger seat. "Are you sure you want to go in?" he asked.

"Without a doubt."

It had been about two months since the horrible events at the summer camp. After Otto killed Eric and untied David, he ran to the camp director's office. He reconnected the phone and called for the police and an ambulance. The ambulance arrived within thirty minutes and took Freddy, Jessica, and David to the hospital for treatment. Jessica was treated for her broken arm and received twenty-seven stitches in her leg. Freddy underwent several procedures that night for his collapsed lung and required a blood transfusion. He was eventually released from the hospital after about two weeks. The police came and rescued the other campers. They found many injuries among the survivors as well as the dead bodies of two children. Over the next couple of days, the police questioned all of the children and counselors and eventually decided to arrest two of the counselors who participated on the red team. All of the remaining children from the yellow and red teams were sent home with no further action. Stories ran all around the world, not just of the horrors of what had happened at Camp Ohiwa but also of the death of Eric Bauer, one of the top Nazi war criminals who escaped at the end of World War II.

The reunion with Otto was full of mixed emotions. Otto had not completely remembered David but would later fill him in that his mother, Emma, had secretly told him the truth about his real father as he grew older. Of course, Otto always felt some allegiance to the only father he ever knew but really began to believe his mother's stories as he saw his dad's behavior at the camp. Eric had treated Emma very badly over the years, and she never had a happy moment. Otto could not remember a single time his mother ever smiled. Eric had beaten her time and again over the years. He kept her locked up in their home. She was never even allowed to go to the grocery store. She lived these years as Eric's slave until one day, her madness became so evident that Eric had her locked up and committed as a psychotic schizophrenic who would make up stories about the war. This was years ago.

For David, he had given up long ago on ever being reunited with Emma or Otto. He spent years searching for them after the war. He even tried to track them down in Argentina and Australia, following endless leads. Apparently, Nazi leaders had escaped to these places, and he did find matching descriptions for the three of them through work with Nazi hunters. But each lead ended in disappointment. He became more depressed than even during his days at Auschwitz because at least then he was able to get a glimpse of them, and there was hope. Now having lost everything, he wandered from city to city, grabbing odd jobs and renting rooms in boarding houses. He eventually took a job as a bus boy at a quaint French restaurant in Paris. One evening, he saw a man he vaguely remembered from years ago. It was Frank Castenbaum, his distant cousin from America, who used to come to Berlin before the war to do business with his father at the bank.

"David? Is that you?"

"Hi, Frank," David said, offering a small smile.

"Oh my God, I have been so worried about you and the family. I haven't heard from anyone since before the war. I have written to your mother and father many times and never got a reply. I feared the worst."

"It is the worst," David said. "They're all dead."

Frank gasped and turned white. "All of them?"

"My mother and father were killed at Auschwitz. My brother was hung from a tree. My wife and child were stolen by a Nazi and seem to have disappeared from the face of the earth. I have wandered the world in search of them. I have nothing left."

"You are coming with me, David," he said, standing up from his chair, tears in his eyes. He pulled David in for a tight embrace, and David lost it. The tears just flowed and he felt as though his legs couldn't carry his weight. He collapsed in his embrace. It took a few weeks to get the documents they would need, but he eventually moved to NJ into his cousin's house along with his cousin's wife, Anne. Frank's three kids had already left home and were starting their lives. It was time to start his life again.

Now, standing outside the psych ward with his long-lost son, David thought about the difficult situation he faced. He had two wives. He loved Ally and their life with his twin boys. They were everything to him. But now, back from the dead was Emma and Otto.

David opened the door, but Otto grabbed his arm.

"Dad, she is not how you remembered. She hasn't spoken in four years. She just stares, and if you get too close, she will attempt to claw at you. She doesn't know me anymore. She is gone."

David nodded.

"I'll wait for you in the lobby," said Otto. "I can't bear to see her anymore. It breaks my heart."

They checked in with the clerk at the front desk. Otto took a seat, and after a few moments, a nurse in a white uniform came out to escort David to see Emma.

"She's in the garden watching the fountain," said the nurse.

They walked on in silence. He was so close to seeing her again. His Emma. They made a few turns and then went through a glass door out to a courtyard where several patients were seated, mostly alone. They looked like zombies. They just stared expressionlessly in front of them. And then he saw her. He only had a partial view of her face, but it was clearly Emma.

"Now, make sure you stay a few feet away. Probably best if you sit across from her on the side of the fountain pool. I will be attending to some of the other patients. Please call me if you need me," said the nurse, who smiled and walked off.

David approached Emma from the side and sat down across from her on the ledge of the fountain. She didn't move or acknowledge his presence. She had changed. Her hair was all white now despite her youth. There were hints of her former beauty. She stared right through him as if he was not even there. He just sat there for a while feeling so sad about what had become of her. Finally, he tried to talk to her.

"Emma, darling. It's me, David. I'm so sorry I couldn't protect you. I left you with that monster. I felt it was the only way I could save you and Otto. I'm so sorry, darling. I can't imagine the horror of being with him all of those years."

Emma never moved but just continued to stare.

"The day Auschwitz was liberated, I came looking for you, but you were all gone by the time I got to Eric's house. I searched the world for you for years after the war. I fell into a deep depression and finally gave up. There was no trace of you or Otto. It was as if you all had just disappeared. There has never been a day that I have not dreamed and prayed that you would return to me." Tears were flowing down his face now. "Oh, Emma, I'm so sorry."

They sat in silence for about twenty minutes. Finally, David got up. "I will never stop loving you, Emma darling." Then he turned and walked away.

"David," said a quiet, hoarse voice.

He turned and saw Emma was looking at him now. She had a single tear running down her left cheek.

"Why didn't you come for me?"

"Oh, Emma," he said, crouching down before her, his hands now cupping her face.

"David, I never stopped loving you either."

He kissed her deeply, and she returned the kiss. And then her mouth went limp, and when he looked up, her blank stare had returned. He tried unsuccessfully to get through to her again, but it wasn't to be.

Over the years, he returned to visit her frequently, but she never spoke or recognized him again. She was gone. She was not one of the six million, but she was gone all the same.

Born in New Jersey in 1980, Roger Coron's childhood bedtime stories usually included history lessons. His father, Mark Coron, a periodontist was born in 1946, would teach him all about American and world history. As a true baby boomer, it was no surprise that his favorite topics included World War II and the Cold War.

History was a passion that Roger and his father shared. When his father died suddenly at the age of 45, Rogers world changed in a minute. At age 11, he was the oldest of three children. On her own, his mother, Jill Coron-Mazzarell raised Roger along with his 9 year old sister, Jennifer and 4 year old brother, Josh.

With the passing of his father, Roger decided to emulate his career but preferred medicine to dentistry. After high school, Roger studied at Vassar College where he majored in biology. In 2002, he was admitted to the University of Medicine and Dentistry of New Jersey. After graduating medical school in 2006, he continued his medical training with an internship and residency at Thomas Jefferson University Hospital and a fellowship in Gastroenterology at the New York Medical College.

In 2022, he moved his family to South Florida and joined the Cleveland Clinic where he practices today. He lives with his wife, Radhika, an anesthesiologist and pain management physician and their two children, Mark and Hunter.

Despite his love for gastroenterology, he never lost his passion for history. Thanks to his mother's guidance, Roger read countless novels on what he considers the most intriguing subject in history, World War II. In 2023, he decided to write his own historical fiction which he published in 2024.